FIRESTORM

By Colin D. Peel

FIRESTORM

COLIN D. PEEL

PUBLISHED FOR THE CRIME CLUB BY
DOUBLEDAY & COMPANY, INC.
GARDEN CITY, NEW YORK
1984

All of the characters in this book
are fictitious, and any resemblance
to actual persons, living or dead,
is purely coincidental.

Library of Congress Cataloging in Publication Data

Peel, Colin D.
Firestorm.

I. Title
PR6066.E36F5   1984   823'.914
ISBN 0-385-19411-0
Library of Congress Catalog Card Number 83–27004
Copyright © 1984 by Colin D. Peel
All Rights Reserved
Printed in the United States of America
First Edition in the United States of America

A knight and a lady
Went riding one day
Far into the forest,
Away, away.

"Fair knight," said the lady,
"I pray, have a care.
This forest is evil;
Beware, beware."

A fiery red dragon
They spied on the grass;
The lady wept sorely,
Alas! alas!

The knight slew the dragon,
The lady was gay,
They rode on together,
Away, away.

Traditional Nursery Rhyme

FIRESTORM

ONE

The picture on one of the TV monitors had begun to flicker.
I bit down on another matchstick, flattening it completely
before I spat it out.

The floodlights were in the wrong places, there weren't
enough of them and without a picture of Compound Three
we had a blind spot that was dangerously close to the river.

Right now anything could be happening out there. I
imagined shadows moving among the pipework and the
tanks. Fingers busy with explosives and detonators smug-
gled onto the peninsula from the Rhine.

The possibilities were limitless. Wearing wet suits and
underwater gear a dozen men could have bypassed the police launches and landed anywhere along half a mile of river
frontage. Maybe they'd done something to the TV camera.
Something clever to screw up the picture on our monitor.
Or maybe I'd just been on the job too long.

Someone else was nervous. A security man who spoke
quietly into his radio before coming to stand alongside me
at the window.

"Please, you will tell me which is Compound Three," he
said. Like most of the Germans in the room, he spoke English with an American accent.

I pointed out towards the end of the peninsula. "The last
eight tanks. The big ones."

He consulted a piece of paper. "Five of them contain fuel
oil and three are empty. Is that correct?"

"More or less. There aren't actually any empty tanks out

there. The three next to the river are filled with water—it's
safer that way."

A fire truck had reached the containment wall, its search-
light glinting on the tanks while the driver probed the compound for anything unusual. I wondered how long he'd be
game to stay there. Straight explosives are one thing but a
bomb in an oil depot is something else. In my two weeks
here at the Duisburg installation I'd learned enough from
the oil men to make me scared of even the smallest tanks.

"Five million litres," the security man muttered.

His calculation was wrong but I didn't tell him. If it was
going to happen, a million litres one way or the other
wouldn't matter much.

Geoff Green came over to join us. He was the only other
Englishman working on the project and the only person in
the room who was smiling.

"You're getting jumpy," he said. "They won't hit Compound Three. Why mess with heavy oil when there's aviation fuel right next door? They'll go for the low-flash-point
stuff."

Geoff was responsible for the seven Claribel units that
had been installed high on the catwalks above the depot. By
instantly tracing the path of a bullet and identifying its firing
point, these little radar sets made sniping a hazardous activ-
ity for terrorists. Tonight, if one of the tanks did blow, radar
would tell us if an incendiary bullet had come from outside
the perimeter. That wouldn't stop a fire but it gave us a
good chance of catching the gunman and it was one way of
finding out whether I'd done my job properly or not.

The TV picture was stable now. It showed the fire truck
crawling back towards us in the shadows of the steel tanks
which made up the huge Rochling installation.

"What do you really think the odds are?" Geoff asked.

"Of keeping the lid on or having the whole lot go up?"
He grinned. "Keeping the lid on."

I wished I had the answer. One after another as they'd
been pumped dry I'd sloshed around inside each of these
twenty-four stinking tanks. Every tank, every foot of
pipework, every valve and every dark hole that could hold a
matchboxful of high explosive had been inspected at least
twice—but still I wasn't sure.

"If there's a bomb out there, one of us brought it in," I
said without conviction.

I could have guessed the German guard would take my
remark literally.

"There had been restricted entry to the depot since the
alert," he said. "Each day everyone has been body-
searched, yet you suggest a bomb has been carried in by a
member of the security force. I do not understand, Mr.
Harwood."

I was tired of talking to Germans. Only Germans could
have moved with such extraordinary speed and efficiency to
protect the installation, but I was weary of the humourless,
stern-faced men who made up the Duisburg antiterrorist
team.

Geoff fielded the question for me. He drew the security
man aside and whispered to him. "Mr. Harwood is worried
about Herr Keller. Have you noticed the large briefcase he
carries?"

The German smiled weakly, excused himself and returned to watch the bank of television screens.

Tonight, twelve people were crowded into the tiny control room. As well as Geoff and me, there were the Duisburg
fire chief and his colleague from Essen, four members of the
Rochling staff and four heavily armed gentlemen from Federal Security. Twelve of us taking care not to be seen looking at our watches too often.

Chain-smoking in the corner, Walter Keller was plainly
anxious. As operations manager of one of the world's larg-

est oil storage complexes, he had more at risk and more to lose than any of us.

It had been Keller who'd phoned me in London, explaining how he'd been given my name by the West German government and then going on to promise substantial quantities of Deutschmarks if I would give up whatever it was I was doing and travel immediately to Duisburg.

I could still recall my doubts while I'd listened to what he'd had to say. Perhaps if I'd had the sense to do some checking, if Keller had been able to tell me the full story over the telephone, or perhaps if the mess with Lisa hadn't been so fresh in my mind, I might have turned him down. But I hadn't turned him down, and, at the time, agreeing to help stop a bunch of Red Army terrorists from setting fire to the Rochling oil depot had seemed like a fairly good idea. A quick, dirty job to help forget Lisa and provide enough cash to get me out of England for the winter. But it was a job I now knew was impossible—not just for a burned-out explosives expert but for all of the other experts who'd been assigned to the project with me. The security police knew it, the German government knew it and, better than anyone, Walter Keller knew it.

I saw him reach for the phone.

Minutes had been dragging like hours but now Keller was to make his final check with the Ministry at Bonn, I found myself hoping something might delay the ten forty-five deadline.

People were looking towards the river where a large white helicopter was hovering mothlike at the far end of the peninsula. Twin beams from its landing lights were streaming out across the tank farm but the pilot was keeping well away from the depot in case the Red Army were better at their job than we were at ours.

In fifteen minutes we'd know who'd won. Keller's call to Operation Headquarters wasn't going to alter anything.

Right at the beginning Bonn had told the Rochling management that bargaining with the terrorists was out of the question no matter how high the stakes and it was foolish to expect the government to change their minds at the eleventh hour.

Nineteen jailed terrorists were going to stay where they were in Hamburg jail and that meant the Red Army leaders had no option but to make good their threat to blow up the depot—or at least try to.

I chewed on another matchstick, waiting for Keller to come off the phone.

He spoke for a further minute, then replaced the receiver very gently. There was no need for him to say anything. From his expression it was clear no one had shifted their position. Negotiations with the Red Army were over.

I felt alone. Unlike Geoff and everyone else in the room, tonight I was nothing but an observer. Downstairs, inside the perimeter, nearly a hundred men were on standby, ready to turn valves, start pumps or flood the compounds with foam if the worst was to happen. Outside the fence, more men in police cars and fire trucks waited for instructions from the people here in the control room but, well done or not, my job was finished. If there were explosives hidden somewhere in the Rochling depot, I hadn't been able to find them and the time for second thoughts had long since gone.

Pausing occasionally to discuss strategy with his compound supervisors, Keller was reading out instructions from his check sheet over his walkie-talkie.

He saw me looking at him and forced a smile. "In your place, Mr. Harwood, I think I would have stayed in my hotel with a bottle."

I didn't tell him the idea had been high on my list. In recent months there had been more hotel rooms and more bottles than I cared to remember.

"I'd need to paint the windows over," I said returning his smile. "My room's on the top floor."

Keller nodded. "If we are unlucky, all of Duisburg will know soon enough. By morning all of Germany will know."

The Essen fire chief said something in German.

Keller translated for me. "Herr Sachsenroder says that should we fail, the next time the government will give in to the terrorists. He believes the Rochling depot will be an expensive test case."

Outside, a siren wailed and lights started flashing on the main console.

Keller grabbed his radio.

My pulse quickened. An attempt to breach the fence or a landing on the waterfront? Either would increase my confidence. Successful or not, a raid from outside the depot was an indication that explosives hadn't been concealed inside.

"Damn," Keller said angrily. "The TV or the newspapers have arrived. Two streets away someone is taking pictures from a crane."

"Good front," Geoff remarked quietly. "You could launch a rocket from a crane."

It was nearly time. Geoff moved off to tend his radar screens while the Rochling engineers started making last-minute checks on their high-speed video recorders.

All conversation in the room had stopped and I could taste the cigarette smoke and the tension.

At ten forty-two there was a sudden flash of light to the south. Seconds later it was followed by a sound like a rifle shot. The explosion was some distance away, well outside the perimeter but loud enough to make my palms sweat.

Struggling to keep his voice calm, Keller was using two radios and a telephone as he tried to discover what had happened.

He was still trying when the top of one of the tanks blew off.

Disbelievingly, I saw a gigantic fountain of aviation fuel gush upwards and outwards over Compound Two. At the same time the side wall of the tank split open allowing a hundred thousand gallons of fuel to spill out into the containment area.

Everywhere people were running and yelling.

High-pressure nozzles started throwing foam towards the waves of fuel washing around the bases of other tanks. But it was too late.

Long before the ruptured tank had emptied, the east windows of the control room shattered and Compound Two was engulfed in orange flame.

People were shouting instructions over the dreadful roaring noise from outside, the control room was in pandemonium and only the video tapes would show how long it was before neighbouring tanks went up.

When they did, flames erupted several hundred feet into the sky, swirling higher and higher until the whole of Compound Two was nothing but a boiling hell of smoke and fire.

For a while the sheer fury of it prevented me from thinking at all and even when at first the truth began to dawn on me I had refused to accept it. But the truth was inescapable. Unless the rifle shot had signalled the launch of something from outside the depot, only a bomb could have triggered disaster on this scale.

I turned to Geoff Green for an answer. Beneath the hand shielding his eyes from the glare his face was grim. Slowly he shook his head.

By now seven fire trucks were blasting foam into the compound while near the office block a separate attack was being mounted by the Rochling staff using three low-expansion foam branch pipes. Joining them the Düsseldorf fireboat was also spraying foam from nozzles mounted on its bow.

Standby fire trucks from the Düsseldorf and Essen brigades raced along the peninsula heading for the heavy-oil compound before vanishing into the pall of smoke now blanketing the depot. Closer to the control room, mobile foam monitors were still being towed into position although most of the tanks in Compound One were already enveloped in water sprays to keep them cool.

To someone who had never seen one, it was impossible to imagine a fire could reach such proportions.

No matter how much equipment was brought in, efforts to extinguish it would be futile. All the foam in the world couldn't control anything so obviously uncontrollable, let alone put it out.

I stood at the window numbed by what I saw—unable to believe my negligence was responsible for all this.

In the control room no one would meet my eyes. Fair-minded men might believe I had tried my best but the destruction of the Rochling depot had been started by something I had overlooked and my best had not been good enough. The Englishman who understood explosives had failed and the bitterness of everyone who had worked on the project with me could not be concealed.

Out on the peninsula superhuman efforts were beginning to take effect. Each minute, thousands of gallons of foam were cascading onto the lake of burning fuel, cooling the surface and keeping oxygen away from the flame. Water from hundreds of fixed nozzles had generated a water curtain around Compound Two and foam jets from the more powerful monitors were arcing over seventy feet into the sky, drenching men who were fighting what was already the worst industrial fire Germany had ever seen.

I watched until a burst tank flange allowed light fuel to escape into Compound One. It caught fire immediately, spreading quickly through broken pipelines into the harbour basin.

Despairingly, Keller ordered a boom to seal off the east-

ern part of the harbour and diverted equipment to the rail-
way embankment. A blazing slick of oil is almost impossible
to fight from the land and Keller knew he was losing.

Everywhere, water-filled tanks that had lost their contents
through buckled and broken pipes were collapsing and
melting. Everything was obscured by smoke and the noise
was unbearable.

I let myself out of the control room. The stench and the
heat hit me like a wall but my senses had gone into overload.
Stepping over hundreds of hoses on my way to the gate I
grew progressively detached from the horror of it all until
the roar behind me no longer mattered.

Once outside the gates it was easy to avoid looking back
and easier to ignore the questions shouted at me by sightseers. I was insensitive to the fire and insensitive to my own
feelings about it—a reflex insulating me from everything
that had happened here tonight.

The streets were choked with people hurrying towards
the river, their faces illuminated by the awful glow from the
depot.

In trying to avoid them I collided with a girl wearing pink
overalls who dropped out of the sky in front of me.

She was winded by the fall but determined not to let me
pass.

"Do you speak English?" she asked breathlessly.

"No," I said.

"Oh good, you do." She brushed off her knees. "I saw
you come from the depot. Was it definitely a bomb?"

The camera gave her away. I glanced up to see a cut-down
oil drum swinging from the jib of an enormous, mobile
crane.

I pushed past her.

"You're Paul Harwood, aren't you?" she shouted at my
back.

I carried on up the street hoping she wouldn't try to follow me.

When I reached the hotel I went directly to my room where I ripped the TV aerial out of the wall and collected two bottles from the wardrobe. The rest of the night was going to be all bad and I had to find a way of getting ready for tomorrow.

TWO

A grey November dawn was leaching colour from the room when I woke up. In the street below someone was banging garbage cans together. I was very cold.

To remind me that nothing had got better in the few hours I'd been asleep, the knot in my stomach was still there.

I retrieved an empty bottle from the floor, dropping it into the wastepaper basket on my way to the bathroom.

The mirror over the washbasin confirmed a need for large amounts of coffee or fresh air. Knowing Duisburg's fresh air to be laced with exhaust fumes at this time of the morning, I settled for coffee, asking room service to send up enough for two.

After I'd turned the air conditioning on to HOT I went to the window and looked in the direction of the Rochling installation. Although it lay three miles away to the east, hidden from view by buildings across the street, in the dark last night the glow from the peninsula had lit up half the town.

Tanks at the depot had held sufficient oil to burn for days on end and, unless sometime in the last eight hours the flames had been extinguished, this morning the sky would be thick with smoke. But the horizon was clear with no sign of the black clouds which I feared might still be rising from the fire. Keller had beaten it after all.

Now it was over I could imagine how the depot looked. A mess of oil, water, twisted steelwork and blackened concrete

—all because of a bomb I was sure had not existed. The feeling of helplessness was back—the same sense of overwhelming guilt I'd experienced last night.

Thoughts of what I should do and where I should go were interrupted by the arrival of my breakfast. I took the tray from the girl and thanked her.

Propped against the jug a folded newspaper told me what I already knew. *ROCHLING DEPOT BRENNT!* the headline shouted.

Below it a large picture showed how well the fire had burned. I poured some coffee, then sat down to examine the photograph. It had been taken from the Rhine side of the peninsula—presumably by someone on the fireboat or by an enterprising photographer who must have hired a launch to get so close.

Scanning the cover story unsuccessfully for the word *"bombe,"* I decided the paper would have gone to press too early for anyone to have issued an official statement on the cause of the fire. Even so, I was surprised that the possibility of a bomb had not been mentioned. Perhaps the reporter had used some other word.

I drank my coffee trying to remember the German for explosives and wondering why it mattered what the hell the paper said.

Last night was just another backward step. First Ireland, then Lisa and now this—a lousy end to the string of bad breaks that in the last year had drained away whatever had been left of my luck.

The phone rang. I expected the inquest to start early but I wasn't ready.

It was Geoff Green. He sounded worried.

"Are you okay?" he asked.

"I guess so. How bad did it get?"

"Compound Two went completely," he said. "They

saved most of the tanks in One and all heavy fuel oil. Bloody incredible."

"Does anybody know what started it?" I said quietly. "For certain, I mean?"

"No." He paused. "Nothing came in from outside. I've been over the tapes twice. I'm sorry, Paul."

"What about the videos covering Compound Two?"

"Keller played them back before he left. They don't show anything we didn't see. Just the top blasting off that first tank."

"Hydraulic pressure," I said. "A straight shock wave."

"That's how it looks."

"Geoff, there wasn't a bomb inside that tank and there wasn't one in the compound, either." I tried to believe what I was saying. "It was something else. Something we missed."

"A couple of the Rochling people said that too—guys that had been working with you."

"But Keller doesn't believe them," I said.

"Doesn't matter whether he does or not," Geoff answered slowly. "He takes the can for the whole thing, anyway."

"Christ," I muttered. I knew how Keller must be feeling.

"Do you want me to come over?"

"No," I lied. "What happens now?"

"No idea. If I hear anything, I'll let you know, though. You going to be there all day?"

"Yeah."

I said good-bye and hung up. Suddenly I knew I couldn't stay here waiting. I had to see the tapes, not to convince myself there had been no bomb but to find anything which would tell me how the Red Army had got one into the tank farm after I had checked it out so carefully.

It was too late to help Rochling and it wouldn't help Keller—but I had to know. Maybe, just maybe, one of the security men was not what he seemed to be. Was a member of the Rochling staff a sleeping Red Army terrorist? The driver of the fire truck who'd inspected the compound when the TV picture failed? By inspecting the tapes—by replaying and reliving the hours and minutes before the fire, could I prove the blame lay somewhere else? And if I did, would it stop me running from myself?

I picked up the phone and dialled the number of the Rochling depot.

Anything was better than pretending the fire need not have happened. If it was my fault, I wanted to know it was my fault, and if it was someone else's—I wanted to know that, too.

"Herr Keller, please," I said to the girl who answered. "This is Paul Harwood."

She replied in German but realised her mistake and switched to English.

"Mr. Keller is not here. He left some time ago."

I thanked her and rang off. As well as being dog tired, Keller would be in no mood to speak to me. But if I backed off now, the result was likely to be a taxi to Düsseldorf and the first plane out to London.

I was part way through the two columns of Kellers in the phone book when the phone rang again.

"Ah, Mr. Harwood, I trust you were awake?" Keller's impeccable English was unmistakable.

"I was about to call you at home," I said.

"Then I have saved you a good deal of trouble. My telephone has been temporarily disconnected. According to my wife, it rang continuously for most of last night."

"Look," I said, "I know you haven't had any sleep and I've got a fair idea what you think about the job I did, but I need to talk to you. Would you mind if I came over to your house?"

"I am not at home, Mr. Harwood. Large numbers of

reporters have gathered outside my house. You have obviously not been bothered by them yet."

"Not yet."

"Then I suggest I visit you at your hotel. I telephoned to say I wished to see you."

"That's fine," I said. "How long will you be?"

"Thirty minutes, Mr. Harwood. Please have some coffee ready. Good-bye."

I said good-bye and replaced the receiver. Although he sounded tired, Walter Keller was as tough as anyone I'd ever met but after last night it was unreasonable to expect our relationship to continue on the same basis—not unless he knew something that I didn't.

I found a clean shirt and laid it on the bed, then went back to the bathroom and turned on the shower. Before Keller arrived I needed to assemble my questions and decide exactly what it was I wanted to do.

No sooner had I stepped into the shower than I heard a banging at the door. Cursing out loud, I wrapped a towel round my waist and went to find out who it was.

Standing in the corridor was the girl who'd been taking photos from the crane last night. In the second it took me to recognise her she smiled and said, "Good-morning."

"Go away," I said.

"I don't mind waiting while you finish your shower."

"I mind—go away."

She waved an envelope at me. "I need to talk to you about the fire."

"Talk to someone else."

The smile slipped. "Please, it's important. I don't want an interview or anything."

Keller was on his way, I had no clothes on and this was not the time to be giving a story to a smart girl reporter no matter how pretty she was.

"Please," she said, "it won't take long."

I shook my head. "Look, you're wasting your time. I don't want to talk to you or anyone else."

Instead of the rush of words I expected, her expression changed and she looked unhappy.

For a moment I wavered. Polished technique or inexperience? In different circumstances I might have tried to find out but right now being misquoted in the local press was the last thing I could afford.

I said, "Sorry," then closed the door gently in her face.

Half an hour when Keller arrived I told him the girl had been here. He seemed uninterested.

His face was grey with fatigue but his mouth was set and Walter Keller was still Rochling's operations manager. He sat down and took the cup of coffee I passed him.

"How old are you, Mr. Harwood?" he asked.

"Thirty-four. Why?"

"I was curious why a young man like you should spend his life working with explosives. You do not strike me as someone who finds it necessary to prove anything either to yourself or to others."

"This is a hell of a time for a question like that. You don't seriously want me to answer it, do you?" I said.

He shook his head. "No."

I refilled his coffee cup. "Geoff Green phoned this morning," I said.

Keller looked at me carefully. "He explained that the video tapes have revealed nothing new?"

I nodded. "It's okay. I'm prepared to admit it was a bomb blast that ruptured the first tank. Last night I wouldn't have done, but that was last night."

"And you therefore hold yourself responsible for thirty million marks' worth of damage, to say nothing of the loss of two lives?"

My stomach lurched. "What happened?"

"The inquest is tomorrow but it will tell us nothing new.

The two men were overcome by fumes and subsequently badly burned. Both died before reaching hospital. It is unnecessary to dwell on the details of the accident."

"I didn't do a sloppy job, Keller," I said quietly. "I'm not that kind of guy."

"Indeed." He paused to light a cigarette. "I have called on you in order to explain something. Several days ago I travelled to Bonn where I spoke at length to senior members of the government. I told them the protection of the Rochling installation could not be guaranteed and suggested that the Red Army would almost certainly succeed despite the precautions I had taken."

"So?" I said.

Keller smiled. "I am saying that neither you nor I should allow ourselves to carry this burden for too long, Mr. Harwood. There can be no safeguards for a tank farm containing twenty million litres of oil when evil men are determined to destroy it. You have done your best and I have done mine. That we have failed is obvious. Whether we have been negligent is another matter. I simply wish to say I am grateful for your efforts."

"Thanks," I said quietly. "Now tell me what you're really doing here."

He stood up and spoke without looking at me. "You are a cynic, my young friend." He turned round. "Just because we have known each other only for a short while, you must not suppose I am unaware of your background."

I didn't say anything.

"You arrived in Duisburg with a troubled mind," Keller continued. "If your reference had been less excellent, I would have sent you back to London immediately."

"So you ran a check on me instead," I said.

He nodded. "And studied you carefully until I was satisfied your recent misfortunes had not impaired your work.

However, since last night I have been concerned about you. I am glad to find I misread some of the signs."

It was hard to believe he had been so concerned but Keller was serious—genuinely serious.

"I'm all right," I said. "Really. But thanks—I mean that." I stood up. "There's something I have to do, though. I need to find out how they did it. I need to know how, Keller."

"So do I, Mr. Harwood. So do I." He stubbed out his cigarette, then reached into a pocket and withdrew a flask. "We will reinforce ourselves against the cold then return to the depot—my car is outside."

"One question before we leave," I said.

Keller nodded.

"That bang we heard—just before the tank went up— what was it?"

He smiled. "The blast from a charge of dynamite one kilometre away. It made an extremely large hole in the Bergedorfer Strasse and completely destroyed an underground pipe which until last year supplied the depot with all its water."

During the short drive to the river I questioned him closely about the water main. According to reports Keller had received earlier this morning, despite the efforts of city engineers, parts of Duisburg were still without water but throughout the emergency the Rochling depot had never been affected. Keller estimated that nearly thirty million litres of foam had been dumped on last night's fire—just about all of it generated from water pumped through a new main pipe that had been driven through to the peninsula only eleven months ago. By chance, or perhaps by sheer good fortune, the terrorists' information had been obsolete —a mistake that had saved two thirds of the installation from certain disaster.

"There is a lesson to be learned," Keller remarked. "A tank farm is only as safe as its water supply. Already I have given instructions to purchase equipment that will allow us to pump river water in large quantities to our monitors." He slowed the car and stopped at the entrance to the depot where an armed guard came over to inspect our passes. He waved us through after Keller spoke briefly to him in German.

Inside the gate the smell of oil grew overpowering and everywhere the ground was awash with an emulsion of oil and water. The mess was indescribable.

As we drove onto the peninsula I could see barges on the Rhine through the gap where once the tanks of Compound Two had been. Some of the tanks in the other compounds were badly discoloured but only one of them had crumpled in the heat.

Keller stopped the car and pointed at the boom which still lay across part of the harbour. "All the oil from the surface must be removed if we are to prevent more contamination from reaching the river. We are using detergents and pumping the slurry into a special holding area but it is a long job." He opened his door, then paused. "Is there anything in particular you wish to inspect?"

"Yes, there is. I want to see what's left of that first tank."

Keller nodded. "I will arrange it. Please wait here."

I got out of the car and went over to stand by the containment wall of Compound Two.

Like saucers, the tops of several tanks lay upside down amongst the wreckage. By shearing off at the deliberately weak weld around the top lip of each tank they were supposed to relieve any internal pressure, but temperatures had been so great that the safety feature had been useless. Not a single tank had escaped. All of them had either ruptured or collapsed, spilling out their contents to fuel the fire. Most of the steelwork was unrecognisable and finding exactly where the fire had started was going to be difficult.

Keller returned carrying gum boots and yellow rain slickers. He was accompanied by a Rochling engineer I had met once before. I shook hands with him and said good morning.

"Herr Molt will show us what he has found so far," Keller said. He passed me a pair of boots and one of the slickers. "I suggest we put these on, it is very dirty in there."

Dragging a small hose behind him, Molt jumped into the compound and led us over to what was left of one of the tanks. It was badly distorted and split open from top to bottom—not along a weld but in a long curve that was characteristic of a pressure burst.

I walked round the tank to inspect the rim at ground level until I found what I was looking for—all the evidence anyone would ever need. A giant fist had smashed against the thin sheet metal—a blow that had not only pushed part of the tank into an impossible shape but driven a four-foot hole right through it. Compression transmitted by the fuel inside had blown off the top of the tank but that hadn't prevented the wall from tearing open. Even if the wall had withstood the shock, there was nothing to stop fuel from escaping into the compound through this gaping hole.

If I'd ever doubted the cause of the fire at the Rochling installation, here was classic proof of what I'd feared the most. Only the detonation of high explosives close to the tank could have created this kind of structural damage.

I straightened up. "Bomb," I said bitterly. "Probably a single charge of gelatine dynamite or something like it. Jesus, I'm sorry, Keller."

He met my eyes. "It is good we came. I prefer to know the truth."

The engineer turned on the hose he was carrying and spoke hurriedly to Keller.

"There is a crater in the concrete," Keller said. "He wishes to show us. It will only take a moment."

I watched while a jet of water scoured an area of concrete

to reveal the outline of a ragged crater. It was a surprisingly large hole but I made no effort to examine it. Keller seemed anxious to leave.

Although, like Keller, I too had sought the truth, there was a difference between us. Because of me, millions of gallons of fuel had been destroyed, over a third of the Rochling depot lay in ruins and two men had lost their lives. I thought I could take the truth, but whether I could handle the guilt was another question altogether.

THREE

Winter had come early to Duisburg. A raw chill hung over the waterfront giving the Rhine a bleak, unwelcoming look. Two days ago I had spent my lunch hour on the riverbank enjoying the sunshine and almost managing to forget what I'd left behind in England. Since then the weather had changed and with it a good deal of other things as well.

For the second time in the last twelve hours I chose to return to the hotel on foot. Although he'd questioned me about my future plans and said he'd phone me later, Keller had seemed to understand why I'd declined his offer to run me back by car. Both of us needed to be alone for a while and Keller in particular was long overdue for some sleep. I'd told him I hadn't made a plan but if I thought of one I'd let him know when he called.

Once away from the depot I started to walk more quickly, partly to keep warm and partly because I knew that some-how or other I had to make last night a turning point. Even before the fire, Keller had been shrewd enough to judge my mood, guessing that the longer I spent dwelling on it the worse things would get. He had guessed what I already knew—if I didn't sort myself out fairly quickly, the downhill slide would soon become too fast to stop.

There was no reason for me to stay in Europe now. Whether I would come to terms with it or not, Lisa was gone. The last two years had produced a blank and I was as free and lonely as I'd been before our lives had crossed.

It was ten o'clock when I arrived back at the hotel. I was

cold enough to justify a drink but wary of any excuse that would postpone the serious thinking I had to do.

"Herr Harwood." Behind the desk on the other side of the foyer a small, stout man shouted at me.

To show him I had my key already I waved it at him.

"*Nein, nein.*" He beckoned.

With some reluctance I went over to find out what he wanted. On previous occasions when this had happened our attempts to communicate had been painful failures.

This morning, fearing an equally futile conversation, I listened dutifully, looked at the ceiling when he pointed and avoided saying anything in case he thought I understood. Interestingly enough, an American fifty-dollar bill featured in the explanation but I was not allowed to touch it. Sensing defeat earlier than usual he stopped and spread his hands.

I said, "*Danke schön,*" deposited a pile of small change on the counter and grinned at him. From a rack beside the desk I helped myself to a selection of airline timetables, then took the elevator to the eighth floor.

Chambermaids were busy changing linen and clearing up breakfast trays at the far end of the corridor. That meant they would have already done my room and I wouldn't be disturbed.

Wondering idly if Lufthansa flew to San Diego and whether San Diego would really be a good idea, I opened the door to find my room already occupied.

Earlier this morning, discovering a girl outside my door had been surprising. To find the same girl inside a few hours later was more surprising still.

She was standing up, clearly embarrassed, with her opening speech forgotten.

"Hello," I said, "for the third time."

"Hello." She blushed. "I've been waiting for you."

"So I see." I closed the door behind me. "How did you

get in?" I held up a hand. "Don't tell me. Fifty dollars and some fast talking, right?"

She nodded. "I said I was your sister."

I couldn't resist a smile. "What's your name?"

"Candy. Candy Stafford."

American dollars and the name Candy didn't add up to a local girl or a local newspaper. And the people in Duisburg didn't speak the way she spoke.

"So who are you working for?" I asked.

"No one. I know you don't want to talk to me, Mr. Harwood and I know it's rude letting myself into your room like this, but I was afraid you might leave Duisburg before I saw you again. You're not going to throw me out, are you?"

"Probably not," I said. "I'm too tired. You'd better sit down and tell me how you knew there could be a fire last night. If you haven't got a good answer, I can always have you arrested on suspicion of arson. You're not the official photographer for the Red Army, are you?"

She smiled awkwardly and sat down on the chair I offered her. "I didn't know there was going to be a fire—not for sure, anyway. I promise you I don't work for the Red Army, though."

"But you know my name and I suppose you know what I've been doing in Duisburg."

"Yes, I do."

I sat down on the bed and studied her more carefully. In place of the pink overalls of last night, today she was wearing jeans and a thick polo-neck sweater. Somehow she didn't look like a journalist and although she'd been clever enough to bribe her way past my German friend downstairs, she was too young and uncertain of herself to be a reporter.

"You're American," I said. "Or Canadian."

"American. But my mother was part German. I speak German fairly well."

"That's nice," I said. "What do you want?"

"I want you to tell me what happened last night." She stared at me. "Everything."

"Are you freelancing for a U.S. magazine or something?"

"No—no, I'm not."

She was answering questions without telling me anything. So far, my questions had been fairly pointless, but she'd made no effort to explain why she was here or even why she was interested in the fire.

"You're not trying very hard," I said.

"That's because I don't know what to say—or how to start, quite."

"Oh," I said. "Did you have any breakfast?"

She shook her head.

"I'll do a deal with you," I said. "We will share toast and coffee while I decide whether I'll tell what happened at the Rochling oil depot. You'll be able to read it all in the paper tomorrow, anyway. But, Miss Stafford, if I do tell you, you are going to have to explain what you want the information for—who you are, why you're here and why you're bothering me instead of someone else."

"I might need more than that," she lowered her eyes. "I know it sounds crazy."

She was right, it did sound crazy, but my curiosity was growing. "What is that supposed to mean?" I said.

"I can't do a deal—not like that. I have to find out more about you first." She looked up. "You see, I think we might be able to help each other. It's just that I don't know yet."

With her last statement our conversation such as it was had taken an unexpected turn. I had absolutely no idea what she was talking about and even less idea what was behind her last remark.

"All right," I said. "First I'll order breakfast, then we'll start again."

While I phoned room service she brightened up—probably because she realised I intended taking the time to find out what all this was about.

"I don't suppose you'd tell me about what happened in Northern Ireland as well?" she asked. "I know you did some work there."

By now I was beginning to appreciate that for some inexplicable reason she'd been digging into the less illustrious parts of my past.

"Why the hell should I do that?" I said. "You aren't even making any sense. What's Ireland got to do with last night?"

"I've told you," she said earnestly. "I have to find out more about you before I can explain properly."

"Okay, okay," I said. "Stop going round in circles."

In the ten minutes she'd been here she'd succeeded in mystifying me thoroughly—not just by asking questions but because of the way she asked them. Even the questions themselves were odd. Her approach was so unsophisticated there could be no doubt it was genuine, and instead of being irritated I was intrigued. That was little enough justification to provide her with information, but it was difficult to see what harm could come from it, especially if she knew the answers anyway. I wasn't so sure I wanted to talk about Ireland, though. Why on earth did she want to know about that and what possible connection could it have with the fire?

I made up my mind. "All right, Miss Stafford," I said. "Now you listen. I'll give you a two-minute rundown on what happened in Northern Ireland. After that, unless you come up with a damn good reason for being here, I'm either going to throw you out or phone the police. I'll only answer questions on the oil depot after I know exactly what this is all about. How does that sound?"

She frowned. "I didn't want to make you angry. You just say what you want to."

It was pointless explaining that nine months of horror in

Belfast were impossible to describe. Twice in the last year I'd blurted out the story to a half-drunk stranger in some godforsaken bar but the process didn't work. Unloading memories onto other people didn't get rid of them and I was still a long way from being able to remember without wishing that I couldn't.

Her expression had changed. "I shouldn't have asked you, should I?" she said softly. "I'm sorry."

"There's nothing to be sorry for," I snapped. "Not any more. There's not even much to tell. You're going to be disappointed. High explosives aren't as exciting as they sound. I've worked with them for twelve years now—military stuff, mining, bombs, demolition—the whole lot. About two years ago I even started believing what people were telling me and thought I was some sort of expert. That was one reason why I went to Northern Ireland—a bad reason. You see the British government invited me to go there. That was the word they used—invited. I was supposed to teach army personnel how to defuse IRA bombs. Because I'd run courses in Europe and the Middle East along the same lines they thought I'd be good at it."

I stood up, unwilling to go on. Why was I telling her this? What right had she to ask me questions about anything?

"What happened?" she said.

"I thought you might have read about it," I answered. "A couple of hungry journalists wrote an article for one of the weekend papers."

She said nothing, waiting for me to continue.

"I'll tell you what happened, Miss Stafford. I spent weeks finding out how clever the IRA are. Pulling fuses to pieces inside cars and buildings while I waited for the one that had been assembled by someone smarter than I was. When I thought I'd learned it all, I started training bomb-disposal teams, going out with them until I was sure they knew what they were doing."

I paused and stared down at her. "Have you any idea what a few months of that kind of work does to you? I trained thirteen teams altogether. Fifty-two men, of whom twenty-six are dead—blown to bloody hell."

She stared back at me. "It wasn't your fault."

"You don't know a damn thing about it—wait until I've finished. There were two instructors helping me. One of them was an explosives expert, too, but I didn't realise that until it was too late. It was the police who found out I'd had a member of the Republican Army working alongside me. The bastards in the IRA learned exactly how I'd deactivate a bomb to make it safe. Once they knew that, all they had to do was booby-trap their fuses the right way. I showed them how to kill twenty-six soldiers, Miss Stafford—twenty-six."

This time she didn't say anything for several seconds.

"You couldn't have known," she said calmly. "It wasn't your job to know."

Before I could answer there was a knock on the door. Breakfast had arrived.

I let the waiter put the tray on the table. While I searched for some marks to tip him I saw his eyes flicker over the girl.

She radiated the kind of innocence men would find attractive, but even though it was hard to believe she could be acting out a part I had no intention of accepting her innocence at face value. At least not yet.

I watched her pour the coffee. "That was Ireland," I said. "Last night was different. How did you know Red Army terrorists had threatened to blow up the Rochling installation? Security was as tight as hell but you went and hired a crane so you could photograph the fire. I've told you about Ireland—now it's your turn."

She smiled slightly. "I've messed it up. Mostly I wanted to know about the Rochling fire—that's the most important thing. You got angry before I could stop you."

"Just talk," I said. "Just talk."

She nodded. "It's a bit complicated, I'm afraid." She handed me a plate.

"I'd better tell you about the island first," she began. "Rough and Ready Island. It's in a deepwater channel near Stockton in California. There's a U.S. naval communications station on the island with an oil storage depot right next door to it. The depot doesn't belong to the Navy but it's very close. Sixteen months ago a scientist at the base was approached by someone from the Soviet embassy in Washington. It turned out the Russians knew the scientist was a practising homosexual and started blackmailing him—they wanted to get their hands on a piece of special equipment the Navy was developing on the island—some kind of sonar, I think it was. Does that sound right?"

I nodded. "Yes."

She went on immediately. "I don't know all the details but apparently the plan was to create a diversion by starting a fire at the oil depot one night so the scientist could get equipment out of the base and into a boat which would be waiting in the channel.

"What the Russians didn't know was that the scientist had gone to the CIA and told them what was going to happen." She paused to drink her coffee. "I imagine he felt guilty or got scared."

Her story was growing more intriguing by the minute but I still had no idea where it was leading nor could I guess why she wanted to tell me all this. "Go on," I said.

"Well, the CIA set a trap, of course. They figured the Russian team would use a boat to fire-bomb the depot from the channel and then wait for the scientist to smuggle the sonar equipment out. The CIA were very serious about it. They put over twenty people into the depot and had patrol launches hidden everywhere. No one dreamed the Russians would get through and set the tanks on fire."

"But there was a fire?" I asked.

"Yes. About half an hour before the scheduled pickup time."

"How?" I asked. "I mean what started it?"

"The CIA said a bomb had been planted in the depot somewhere." She stared at the table. "Four tanks went up—over a million gallons."

"Did they catch anyone?" I said.

She shook her head. "Only the man from the Soviet embassy who'd been blackmailing the scientist. The boat never showed up."

"Hell of a story," I said. "Where does Candy Stafford fit into all that?"

"My father was in charge of the oil depot." She looked up suddenly. "It was his responsibility to make sure the tanks were safe."

A glimmer of light had appeared at last. Perhaps more than a glimmer. "Are you going to tell me he was convinced there hadn't been a bomb at the tank farm?"

She nodded. "That's right. To make certain he spent two weeks taking photographs and going over the wreckage. Then he wrote a report showing how the fire must have started. That's when the oil company sacked him. Now are you beginning to see why I'm here?"

"I think so. What happened next?"

"My father started collecting reports on other fires—not just fires in oil depots but at all sorts of other places as well. He used to shut himself up for days on end while he was reading. He travelled all over the States talking to people, too."

"And then?" I prompted.

"Then, Mr. Harwood, one evening when he was driving back from San Francisco, someone ran him off the road and killed him."

I frowned at her. "Do you know that for sure or are you guessing? What did the police say?"

"The police said it was an accident. Lots of car accidents in California are just accidents—especially when a car burns to the ground so there's no evidence left. My mother eventually accepted it but I didn't."

"Why not?"

"Because twelve days afterwards our house was broken into and all my father's notes were taken from his desk."

My coffee had gone cold. What she'd told me was an extraordinary account of espionage, blackmail and the reason behind a fire that had taken place six thousand miles away. If I equated terrorism in Germany with espionage and blackmail in the U.S., I was left with two fires—one in California and one in Duisburg—both caused by bombs that hadn't been there. But Candy Stafford wasn't sitting in my hotel room because of that coincidence. I hadn't told her about last night and she couldn't know yet what had caused the destruction of the Rochling tank farm.

"That doesn't explain why you're here," I said.

"I'm here because you're here. I followed you." She stood up and went to stand in the middle of the room with her back to me. "I've got the names of three people," she said. "Three men who are supposed to know more about explosives than anyone in the world. You're one of them."

"I don't think you've been doing your research in the right circles," I said. "Your information's lousy. But so what?"

"So I was looking for you in England—just before you flew out to Duisburg. I missed you by a day."

"Then you really did follow me to Germany?"

"Yes. Once I got here I started asking more questions. I told you I speak reasonably fluent German. It took me four days to find out Red Army terrorists had threatened to blow up Rochling depot. After that it was easy." She swung round to face me. "I even knew the deadline was last night. In a way everything's worked out rather well—I know that sounds awful considering what happened at Rochling, but it's made you listen to me. If I'd seen you first in London, you wouldn't have believed anything I said."

"Am I expected to guess what you want me to believe?" I asked. "Or are we going on with the game?"

"You can guess, if you like," she smiled at me. "It's not very hard."

I lay back on the bed and thought for a moment before I answered.

"I'm not in the mood for games," I said.

"How about this for a clue?" she said. "I can almost guarantee no one threw a bomb into the depot last night but I'll bet you it was either a bomb or a package of dynamite that started the fire."

I shook my head. "Which means you think it was hidden some time before last night in a place where no one could find it. You're wrong—I had a team of people searching every inch of that tank farm—every day for over a week."

She came and sat beside me on the bed. "Not just hidden. Buried." Candy Stafford had enormous eyes and they were wide open.

Gradually the impact of her statement began to filter through. I sat up. "You can't know that for certain," I said.

"No, but it fits the pattern of fires and bomb blasts my father was working on. You see, I read all his notes before they were stolen—every page. Now will you tell me about last night? Am I right about the bomb?"

I didn't answer her. The position of the crater I'd seen this morning with Keller—where was it in relation to the tank? Could a bomb have been buried under the concrete? My mind was racing. Was this an explanation? Or was I too eager to seize upon anything—even a story as unlikely as the one this girl was offering?

"Mr. Harwood?" she asked.

"Why did you ask about my work in Ireland?" I asked.

She lowered her eyes. "To try and find out what sort of person you are. I couldn't think of another way."

"Why's it important?"

"Because I need someone to help me. Someone who knows about explosives and someone I can trust. Please, Mr. Harwood, tell me if it was a bomb last night."

"It was."

"And could it have been underneath the concrete?" She looked up. "Could it?"

"Very easily," I breathed. "Very easily."

FOUR

This time I didn't walk to the depot. Candy's rental BMW was faster and there was a lot to do before I spoke to Keller again this afternoon.

I jammed on the brakes at the Rochling main gate, waving my pass out the window before the car had stopped. A guard came over. He was carrying a submachine gun.

"Harwood," I said. "You know me."

He looked at Candy through the windshield. "It is not permitted," he said in passable English.

"Okay," I said. "She'll wait here. I'll take the car in and collect her on my way back."

Candy started to get out but the guard was shaking his head.

"The depot is closed, Herr Harwood. I have instructions. It is too dangerous."

"Talk to him in German," I said to Candy. "Tell him it's important. Say Keller sent me."

The guard had understood what I'd said. He became slightly officious. "It is not permitted," he repeated. "There is an accident with the pumping."

I sensed I wasn't going to win. With so many broken pipes it was more than likely there'd been a minor spill in one of the compounds. Until it was cleared up, every extra person in the depot increased the danger of a spark and another fire.

"We'll have to come back later," I said to Candy. "I'll run

you to your hotel and then go and get the tapes. Provided Geoff's got copies, he won't mind me borrowing them.''

I told the guard I'd phone in later, then reversed away from the gate and turned the car round. Although it was frustrating not to be able to examine the crater again, it would still be there this afternoon. In fact, I doubted whether I'd learn much from a hole in the ground, but because the crater had been so close to the rim of the tank, by taking measurements I could perhaps calculate the strength of the blast and determine exactly where it had come from. Now that would have to wait. In the meantime, there were two other pieces of evidence I wanted to see— the photographs Candy had taken from the crane and the video tapes which would show the explosion in slow motion. Pictures wouldn't prove the existence of an underground bomb, but with any luck I might be able to pick out bits of flying debris and get a fix on things from that.

"Is it all right if I borrow your car?" I asked.

She nodded. "While you fetch the tapes, I'll collect my photos—I just hope they've been developed. I took them to one of those overnight places."

"Where's your hotel?" I said.

"Keep going south, then take the Krefeld turn-off. I'll tell you where." She swivelled round in her seat. "You do believe I'm right, don't you?"

"I think there's a chance, yes. For the life of me I can't see how terrorists could have buried a bomb in the depot, but I haven't got any other ideas." I glanced at her. "That's what bothers me. Right now I might believe anything—just to get myself off the hook. I'm probably looking for an excuse."

"Don't forget that wasn't the reason I came to see you, Mr. Harwood," she said. "I told you at the hotel, I want you to help me."

I stopped the car at some traffic lights.

"Help you carry on what your father was doing, you mean?"

She nodded. "I can't go on by myself. I've been trying and I can't."

After the lights changed, I drove more slowly than before.

"You haven't told me a hell of a lot about it," I said.

"You didn't let me. All you can think about is last night's fire. I know that's important but there have been lots of other fires—the ones my father was working on. You haven't even asked me about them."

"What do you expect?" I answered. "I've got a few things on my mind—two men were killed at Rochling."

"So you've added them to the twenty-six in Ireland. You believe you're responsible for the deaths of twenty-eight men. I don't think that's very sensible and anyway it isn't a question of guilt or whose fault it was. Of course you're upset about last night—I understand how you feel—but there's a lot more to it than that. Can't you see? More than a single fire in America and another one here in Germany."

I drew over to the kerb and switched off the ignition.

"Look," I said patiently. "Neither of us knows it was a buried bomb that caused the Duisburg fire—not yet. And your father couldn't have been sure about the one in Stockton, either. An underground explosion is only a plausible explanation so long as you don't start thinking how the bomb got there in the first place. Your father was probably looking for an excuse just like I am."

Her eyes were flashing. "He had the proof," she said angrily. "Information that got him murdered."

"You can't connect Red Army terrorists in Germany with communist espionage agents in California," I said. "They haven't got anything to do with each other."

"You're interested enough to find out if I'm right about last night."

"I hadn't thought of an underground blast before, that's why."

"Will you help me or not?" She was frowning.

This wasn't the time to explain that crusades weren't my line of business. Intrigued though I was by what she'd told me, it was the fire at the depot which occupied my thoughts. Even if by some means or other the terrorists had managed to conceal a bomb beneath the surface of the compound, I couldn't believe that linked it with fires elsewhere. An attractive idea, maybe, but an idea that didn't hang together.

"Let's do one thing at a time," I said. "How about waiting until we've seen the video tapes and your photographs?"

"You're stalling. I didn't think you'd be like that."

I restarted the engine and pulled out into a stream of cars and trucks. For the rest of the journey, she sat tight-lipped in the passenger seat, pointing out the route to her hotel in silence.

It wasn't until we reached the back streets of Krefeld that she spoke again.

"Down there," she said suddenly. "Where that red car's going."

"I'm sorry if you're disappointed," I said. "I'd like to be more enthusiastic."

"I expected you to be interested, not enthusiastic. What are you going to do if I'm right about the bomb at the depot?"

"Tell Keller."

"Then what?"

"See what he wants to do about it."

"There's my hotel." She pointed at a building on the other side of the street. "Perhaps Mr. Keller would listen to me. Do you think he would?"

I made a U-turn and parked the car behind a white Volkswagen Kombi. "He might," I said. "But he'll have the same problem I have. It's hard to connect Duisburg with Stockton, Candy."

Her eyes flashed again. "Not Stockton—not just Stockton. My father investigated fires in New York and explosions in airline terminals and lots of other places—all caused by bombs people said couldn't have been there."

"Okay. We'll talk about it later," I said. "I'm not stalling —really I'm not. It's just that I have to be sure what happened here before I can start thinking about other people's problems."

"You'll bring the tapes, though, won't you? You will come back?"

"Of course I will." I'd given the wrong impression. I wasn't uninterested in her story, nor had I any intention of leaving things where they stood. At the very least I wanted the opportunity to ask her some more questions.

"Look," I said. "Give me a chance. I had a hell of a night and you only sprung this on me a few hours ago. I'll be back as soon as I've got the tapes."

"All right." She opened the car door. "I'm sorry I'm impatient. I've been waiting so long to talk to someone who might understand."

"If Geoff hasn't got copies, I'll have to ask Keller," I said. "That'll take more time, so don't start worrying if I'm late getting back."

She climbed out, then turned and spoke to me before she closed the door. "There's a map in the glove compartment. The phone number of my hotel's written on the front somewhere. I'm in room 818. Would you call me if you're going to be very late?"

I smiled at her. "Promise."

She waved good-bye as I pushed the BMW out to join the lunchtime traffic.

Forty minutes later I arrived at the hotel where Geoff Green was staying. With the help of Candy's map, somehow or other I'd managed to get myself on the wrong side of the Rhine and it wasn't until I reached Duisburg that I'd been able to cross over and thread my way through the back streets.

I parked the BMW outside and tried to decide how much I should tell Geoff.

Because Geoff's company was picking up the bill, his hotel was more opulent than mine. I'd been here only twice and I couldn't remember his room number.

"Mr. Green," I said to the girl at the desk. "Would you see if he's in, please? My name's Harwood."

She checked for his key, then phoned through to his room.

"There's a Mr. Harwood to see you," she said.

"He will meet you in the bar," she said when he rang off. "Through the glass door over there."

I thanked her and went to buy myself a scotch.

By the time Geoff joined me I was on my second one.

"What are you drinking?" I asked.

"Scotch, thanks." He grinned. "You look as though you're ahead of me. Have you been at it since breakfast?"

"If I'd started that early, I wouldn't be here talking to you."

"Keller said you went to the depot with him this morning," he said. "He phoned me a couple of hours ago. It sounds as if they've still got trouble down there."

"Looks like a bomb site," I said. "How's that for an answer?"

Geoff looked sideways at me.

"I hear there's a bloody great hole in the ground."

"There is," I said. "That's what I want to talk to you about. Do you remember the alarm going—just before the water main was blown?"

He nodded. "Some bastard taking pictures from a crane or something."

The barman came over to take my order. I asked him to bring two doubles.

"It was a girl," I said. "She came to see me this morning."

Geoff raised his eyebrows but said nothing.

"She has this theory of a bomb being buried in the compound," I said. "I know it doesn't make sense but I've decided to check it out."

Geoff took one of the glasses and swirled the ice around in it. He kept his eyes on the drink. "Paul, no one could've got into the depot to dig a hole. Why not just leave things alone?"

"If it wasn't for the girl, I would."

He took a long drink. "It's a pound to a pinch of shit they came in from the waterfront and dumped the bomb in the dark. We all knew how vulnerable we were because of the river. Either that or it was an inside job."

"Do you believe that?"

He glanced up. "What the hell does it matter what you or I believe?"

"It matters to me. I've come to ask if you'll lend me the tapes. I want to see exactly where the blast came from."

"You know where it came from—you've seen the crater. You're welcome to the tapes, Paul, but they won't help. Why listen to some crazy story from a girl who's working for a newspaper?"

I could try explaining that Candy wasn't a reporter and tell Geoff everything she'd told me but it would still sound ridiculous. Maybe he was right. People less sympathetic than Geoff would never accept the concept of a buried bomb—especially if I was the person proposing it. Without solid evidence to support the theory, no one would listen and I knew that kind of evidence did not and could not exist. In the absence of proof, perhaps I wouldn't even be able to convince myself.

"I'd like to see the tapes, anyway," I said. "Call it a long shot."

"You're going to be disappointed." He put his room key on the bar. "They're in the top drawer in the cupboard beside the bed. Have you got something to play them on?"

"I'll pick up a deck and a monitor from a hire outfit."

He nodded. "There's one on Duisburg High Street, opposite the garage. You could save yourself the trouble by using the equipment at the depot. Keller wouldn't mind."

"I want the time to take a good look," I said.

"And time to show them to your girl friend? I hope you know what you're doing, Paul. Don't forget who the tapes belong to. They're not yours, they're Rochling's."

I'd worked long enough with Geoff to know he wasn't trying to needle me. He thought I was making a fool of myself, but he wasn't prepared to say so—probably because he felt sorry for me.

"I'm not going to do anything stupid," I said. "And I'm not on a witch-hunt, either. Whichever way you look at it, last night had to be my fault, but I might as well be sure how it happened."

He raised his glass to me. "Go to it, friend. It was a lousy job, anyway. Even Keller knew we couldn't win. Let me know if there's anything you want me to do. I'll be around for a couple more days."

"I'll bring the tapes back tonight. Will you still be here?"

He grinned. "Where else?"

To make certain he didn't run out, before I left I bought a bottle of Teacher's and put it in front of him on the bar.

A few minutes later, when I was on the way out of the hotel with the tapes, the doorman gave me a note. It said *"Nil Illegitimum Carborundum,"* and in case I didn't recognise the handwriting it was signed "Geoff." The message made me smile. So long as there were people like Geoff Green around perhaps the bastards wouldn't grind me down after all.

Outside, feeling more cheerful, I stowed the cassettes in the glove compartment and started the BMW. It was a responsive car to drive, its acceleration allowing me to overtake trucks two at a time in a long, exhilarating surge of power. My spirits, I thought, were on the rise at last.

Diverting only to collect a video deck and a monitor from the shop in downtown Duisburg I was soon heading back to Candy's hotel.

This time I managed to avoid getting lost, arriving in Krefeld shortly after two-thirty.

I parked the car in the same place, unloaded my equipment onto the sidewalk, then balanced the four video cassettes on top of it and carried the whole lot up the steps to the hotel entrance.

Inside a porter came to my assistance by holding open the door of the elevator. He accompanied me to the eighth floor and carried the monitor along to room 818 for me.

Because Germany is awash with pornographic video and because the porter must have known whom I was visiting, he had adopted a knowing expression. I winked as I gave him the tip.

When he'd gone I knocked gently on the door.

There was no answer until I knocked again—harder this time.

"Who is it?" I heard Candy ask.

"Paul Harwood. I've got the tapes."

The door was wrenched open, something smashed across my face and two men pulled me headlong into the room.

FIVE

The blow had been to prevent me from shouting. By slamming the barrel of an automatic pistol hard against my head as soon as the door opened, my silence had been guaranteed.

It felt as though a spike had been driven through my skull and when I lifted a hand to touch my cheek it came away a sticky red.

I stayed on my knees, fighting the pain while I tried unsuccessfully to think.

Very slowly I raised my head. My left eye wasn't working too well but what I could see confirmed my worst fears.

There were three of them. Three of them and Candy. She was standing in a corner, both hands clamped over her mouth and her eyes wide with terror.

The man with the gun trod on my hand. "Get over there with the girl," he said.

I was too dizzy to stand up unaided, and if he hadn't let Candy help me, I wouldn't have made it. She led me to the bed and sat down close beside me. I could feel her trembling.

For a second—for part of a second—I'd thought Candy was part of it. Part of a trap I walked into. But there was no earthly reason why anyone should want to trap us. Not me and not Candy, either. Pain had given way to a numbness extending over half my head but I still couldn't think properly.

"Bring the stuff inside." The same man gave the instruction. He was uniformly large, standing well over six feet and, like his companions, clearly of oriental stock.

While the video equipment was carried in from the corridor, he came to stand in front of Candy.

"Who did you say you were getting these tapes from?"

Candy opened her mouth but nothing came out.

"Green," I said thickly. "Geoff Green."

"Has Miss Stafford been talking to him as well?"

The question implied that all this was the result of Candy's call on me this morning. It might also mean that anyone else Candy had visited was in trouble, too. I was relieved to find the ability to reason hadn't deserted me entirely.

"Geoff Green doesn't know anything," I said.

It hardly seemed worthwhile explaining that I didn't know anything either. Nothing Candy had told me could possibly account for what was happening and until things became clearer I only had one option. Play along with whoever these people were while I tried to find out what the hell was going on.

"So you're the Englishman Rochling hired?" the large man said. "You handle explosives, do you, Mr. Harwood?"

Candy's leg pushed gently against my own. Because I guessed they'd have forced her to tell them who I was, I interpreted it as a signal to say yes.

"I work with them sometimes," I said.

"What precisely has Miss Stafford told you?" he asked. There was the merest trace of a lisp, but the accent, if I could detect one at all, was part American and part English.

Unless I could turn the question into one that required a yes or no, Candy couldn't help me.

"About what?" I said.

A faint smile appeared on his lips. "Mr. Harwood, do not underestimate me. In my business I occasionally meet over-eager men who are blinded by dedication to their particular cause. Some are unreliable and many endeavour to be devious in their dealings with us. I have yet to meet one that is stupid, however. I do not believe you are stupid and you should not suppose that I am. Whether you answer my questions or not is of little consequence. By choosing to answer with Miss Stafford's assistance you are only succeeding in making yourself appear foolish."

"Who the hell are you?" I asked.

"That is unimportant. Miss Stafford may be able to enlighten you. I'm sure she has been trying to answer the same question. You are free to talk to each other while we set up the video equipment you have brought." He slid the automatic into a holster inside his jacket and went to help the others.

It was difficult to reconcile his manner with the brutal way he'd used his gun a moment ago. All round the world I'd met articulate, well-educated men who used violence as readily as they used words. Without exception they'd been confident, ruthless and above all efficient. And here in Candy's hotel was another of the same breed. Where he had come from and what he wanted were parts of a puzzle I couldn't begin to solve, but of one thing I was certain. Concealed beneath this smooth exterior was a cold-blooded killer. Oriental, Caucasian or black African—it didn't matter. I'd seen enough of them to recognise one when I saw one.

Unless this was a crazy accident, I'd stumbled into something far more dangerous and vastly more complicated than the terrorist bombing of the Rochling depot and I was conscious of a growing sense of fear.

"Candy," I whispered, "for Christ's sake, what's all this about? Who are these people?"

"I don't know." Her voice was unsteady. "They knocked on the door about ten minutes after I'd got here. I thought it was you. They just pushed their way in."

"They haven't hurt you, have they?"

She shook her head. "I told them you were coming back —I didn't know what to do—I was so scared. I tried to scream once but I couldn't."

I took hold of her hand. "Candy," I said quietly. "Why do they want to see the tapes? What did they say?"

"They asked me my name and where I came from." She hesitated. "I think it's me they want, not the tapes."

"Do you think they knew who I was—before you told them my name, I mean?"

She nodded. "They knew I'd taken pictures of the fire, too."

"What else did they ask you?"

She looked at me helplessly. "Nothing else." Tears appeared in the corners of her eyes.

I squeezed her hand. "Come on. We've got to figure who they are and why they're here. They must've asked something else."

"Only if I was Desmond Stafford's daughter."

So that was it. Desmond Stafford, Candy's father, who'd spent the last sixteen months of his life trying to prove a theory he had about underground bomb blasts. Maybe he really had been onto something—something so important that by attempting to carry on with his work, Candy herself had become a threat to these people. And if I was right, not only had Desmond Stafford been murdered because of what he'd discovered but now the same people were after his daughter. The idea was all the more shocking because I'd only half believed what Candy had told me this morning. No matter how impossible it sounded, maybe somehow or other a connection did exist between the Rochling fire and similar disasters in other parts of the world.

"Candy," I whispered. "How did they know you were here?"

The large man overheard my question. He loaded one of the cassettes into the video deck before walking over to us.

"We came across Miss Stafford by sheer good fortune, Mr. Harwood," he said. "I shall explain. The circumstances may interest you. Three months ago my company erroneously concluded that Miss Stafford was unlikely to cause us a problem. As a result of her father's foolish meddling we had been following her movements for some time in the United States, but when it became obvious she knew little about our operations, our surveillance was discontinued in July. Then, last night, very much to our surprise, she was recognised by one of my men in Duisburg. Her presence in Germany made us realise our intelligence had been faulty and that we had been wrong in believing her interference would not continue."

It was too early to guess what he was going to do about it, but just recalling the way she'd said her father had died was making my heart thump. I wasn't surprised Candy had been spotted last night. Even before the fire started no one who'd been outside Rochling's main gate could have missed seeing a girl photographer swinging sixty feet from the ground on the end of a crane jib. And, if that's where she'd been recognised, one of our oriental friends had been outside the depot at the same time.

"Miss Stafford came to Germany to talk to me," I said. "Not for any other reason. She only heard about the Rochling scare by accident." Ironically, the truth sounded unbelievable.

"I am not interested in explanations, Mr. Harwood. Explanations are irrelevant. You and Miss Stafford represent a risk and I run a company that does not and cannot take risks. Our business is founded almost entirely on that single principle."

"What business is that?" I asked quietly.

"You already have the answer. I imagine you were at the

depot when the fire began. Our business should be more evident to you than to the other expensive people Rochling hired to safeguard their oil."

"You start fires," I said. "Is that it? You're a German Red Army terrorist?" Nervousness kept the sarcasm from my voice.

The slight smile flickered on his face for a moment. "Not exactly, Mr. Harwood, not exactly. I trust I do not look like one."

I ignored the remark. "What about the tapes?" I asked. "Supposing Candy had turned over another stone and uncovered a bit more of your dirty business, whatever the hell it is, why do you want to see the tapes and where do I fit into things?"

He regarded me coldly, the smile gone. "You do not fit, as you call it. We have assumed Miss Stafford has been foolish enough to confide in you—tell you of her suspicions and tell you what she learned from her father. You, Mr. Harwood, are therefore as dangerous to us as she is. We are not interested in the tapes, but as you have delivered them to us we will take the time to study them. If they reveal too much, we shall take steps to destroy these and other copies but I'm confident that will not prove necessary. Video tapes are of limited value when examining the propagation of shock waves, in our experience."

Apart from learning that Candy and I posed a threat to an organisation of which I knew nothing, I was as much in the dark as I'd been when they'd dragged me into the room. But Candy's suspicions were right. It was not the tapes but Candy they wanted. And, if I'd ever had any doubts, which I hadn't, I now knew both of us were in very deep water indeed.

There was another question I had to ask. I didn't want to ask it and until now I'd avoided the subject but I couldn't put it off forever.

"So what do you want from us?" I asked.

"Nothing, Mr. Harwood. Or, if you prefer a more direct answer, the freedom to carry on our business without the complication or inconvenience you could cause us in the future. Will that do?"

"No, it won't." I paused. "What happens next?" I could feel the sweat running down inside my shirt.

He stared at me. "I thought that would be obvious to you. Despite the crude methods employed to keep you silent when you arrived we are not uncivilised—you will experience no pain whatever. We have special drugs. It will be very quick."

My stomach lurched. Beside me Candy had grown rigid. Unbelievably, the statement had been free of malice. A dispassionate statement from a man who valued life so little that it was of no significance to him.

A hundred times I'd cut through a wire on a fuse that had been too ingenious—a hundred seconds with blood roaring in my ears unable to put off the commitment any longer. But this was different. This wasn't a decision I'd be forced to make. Not a choice whether to live or die but a death sentence at the whim of a stranger.

Still gripping Candy's hand I rose to my feet. "Who the hell do you think you are?" I shouted. "You're out of your bloody mind. This is Europe. Not some goddamn country where people behave like animals. Blow up all the bloody oil tanks you want, but leave us out of whatever rotten business it is you're in. We don't know the first thing about it and we don't want to know. You can have the tapes and you can dynamite every oil depot in Germany, if that's what you get paid for—we aren't involved—do you hear me—Candy and I aren't a risk. Not to you or your lousy company. We don't know anything."

Seeming not to have heard what I'd said, he had continued staring at me during my outburst.

For a moment I considered jumping him—now—while the adrenalin was keeping me on my feet. His gun remained holstered, but even though the other men might not be armed, I was in no shape to take on anyone.

"Have you finished?" he asked.

I couldn't answer. Bewildered and unable to believe this was really happening, I was facing a situation which had assumed the qualities of a nightmare. Unless I could somehow get my message across, Candy and I weren't just in trouble. We were dead.

As if from nowhere the gun appeared. "Get in the bedroom," he said curtly. "You will wait there, and if you think I won't shoot you, Mr. Harwood, you are wrong."

Candy stood up and grabbed hold of me.

One of the other men went to open the bedroom door. His face was expressionless and he, too, was carrying a gun. A small scar disfigured one side of his chin.

I squeezed Candy's hand. "It's okay," I said. "Do what they say."

There was a brief exchange of words in Chinese or Japanese while we were escorted to the bedroom. The man with the scar accompanied us inside and closed the door behind him.

The last vestiges of colour had drained from Candy's face and she wouldn't let go of me. "They're going to kill us," she whispered. "Dear Jesus, they're going to kill us."

From the other room I suddenly heard Keller's voice over the television speaker. There were four video tapes, each recording the onset of the fire from a different camera position. Playing all of them right through would take about twenty minutes but an inspection of the sections covering the instant of the explosion wouldn't take long at all. Five minutes maybe, or less.

Escape was impossible. Fifteen feet behind us, double windows opened onto a tiny concrete balcony but we were eight floors up and German hotels were rarely, if ever, equipped with exterior fire escapes. Candy was paralysed with fear and although I was slowly regaining my strength, we'd stand little chance against armed professionals.

But I'd no intention of waiting for a needle and no illusions about the need to act swiftly. I had four minutes to do something—anything that would stop the unthinkable from taking place.

The guard had taken up a position near the door. Holding his gun loosely he radiated a confidence that looked unnervingly real.

"Do you speak English?" I said.

I pointed at the washbasin. "I need some water, I don't feel too good."

"I'll get it," Candy said.

"No, just help me over there and get my head under the tap."

The muffled roar of an explosion filtered through the door. A minute afterwards I heard the click as the first tape was stopped. Time was running out. Already a quarter of it had gone.

Provided he stayed where he was, moving to the washbasin would bring me closer to the guard. Closer than he'd allow me to approach if I walked directly towards him.

Leaning on Candy, I stumbled heavily across the room. When I reached the washbasin I grasped a tap in each hand, pretending to hold myself up.

A small glass, a toothbrush, a half-used tube of toothpaste and an aerosol can of hairspray—weapons on which our lives depended.

Frantically I searched for a plan—anything to give me the slightest edge. Shortly before I turned on one of the taps I heard the explosion on the second tape.

There was no time left. A few minutes from now they'd be coming for us.

I began sagging, mumbling unintelligibly and struggling to stay upright.

"For God's sake, don't pass out," Candy gasped. "Paul, please. Oh God!" She leaned over to support me.

"Balcony," I whispered.

Then I allowed myself to collapse, sweeping everything off the washbasin on my way to the floor. As my knees touched the carpet I hurled the can of hairspray and launched myself at the guard's feet. "Go," I yelled at her.

His reflexes were too good. A bullet grazed my shoulder and he kicked out savagely at my head.

But before he could fire again I seized his foot and unbalanced him.

Again the muzzle of the automatic spat at me. And again somehow I escaped. Summoning all my remaining strength I heaved and twisted.

Then I was on top of him fighting for my life.

He was stronger than I was but the gun was sandwiched between us and this time he wasn't quick enough. Clamping one hand on the breech and the other on the grip, I squeezed.

The bullet caught him under the chin and tore half his face away.

Still on the floor I ripped the gun from his fingers, pumped a second shot in the direction of the lounge, then sprang wildly towards the balcony. Candy had the door open ready.

The balcony itself was barely wider than the doorway. Pressing against the guard rail on one side, Candy was shielded by less than eighteen inches of concrete from what was sure to come. On the other side where I pushed back against them, the railings were cold on my legs.

Steadying the gun against the doorframe, I waited for the inevitable. The exertion had made me dangerously dizzy and my courage was fading fast. After the gunshots the eighth floor would be in a bloody uproar, but there was still time for the two men to finish things before they took off.

The bedroom door flew open and a million bullets hammered against the wall. Chips of concrete and bits of lead ricocheted past my face. Somehow or other, while more bullets screamed out over the balcony, I managed to squeeze the trigger of my own gun. It kicked twice, adding to the dreadful noise of men trying to kill each other at close range.

When the silence came I wasn't ready for it. It was too quiet, much too quiet.

Dropping to a crouch, Candy poked her head round the corner. I yelled at her to get back.

Gun ready, I eased myself forwards. By now someone in the hotel would have called the police and we had to be safely away from here before they arrived. If it was a trap, there was only one way to find out.

I began counting under my breath.

When I reached ten I made my decision. "Get ready," I said quietly. "Stay exactly where you are until I say it's okay to move."

I stepped back into the bedroom with my gun trained on the doorway leading to the lounge. The smell of cordite was very strong and the silence was overpowering. I felt sick.

But even before I reached the other room I knew they'd gone.

"Come on," I shouted to Candy. "Quickly."

On her way from the balcony she stopped at the body of the dead man. I saw her wrench something from the inside pocket of his jacket.

"Don't be so bloody stupid," I shouted. "There isn't time. Unless we get out of here in the next ten seconds we'll be on a murder charge. Come on!"

She picked up a flight travel bag, then joined me at the front door to the apartment. Her eyes no longer reflected terror but her face was deathly pale. "There's a service elevator," she said. "Turn right in the corridor."

"The bastards might be waiting for us in the corridor," I said, "or in the car outside. We're not out of this yet. When I open the door, follow me and go like hell. We'll make a run for it. If you see anything yell at me—I've still got the gun."

She nodded.

I yanked open the door, pulled Candy out after me and started running.

No shots echoed after us; no bullets in the back and not a sign of anyone.

In a few short hours, my whole life had been turned upside down. Incredibly, both of us were still alive but because of what had happened this cold November afternoon, from here on, as well as the men who had come to kill us, half the Duisburg police force would be on our trail.

SIX

Outside the hotel where I'd left it, the BMW had all the innocence of a loaded shotgun. Or would the danger come from one of the other cars parked along the street? Sprint across to the BMW? Or walk away from it hoping we'd chosen the right direction. The wail of sirens made the decision easy.

"We take the car," I said. "Let me go first so I can unlock it." I gave Candy the gun. "You'll have to cover me. Can you use one of these?"

Doubt was written all over her face but she nodded. "I'll try." She hid the gun behind her handbag.

"When you see me get in, start running," I said. "Don't go to the wrong side."

I got the key ready. "Okay," I said. "See you in a minute."

She put her hand on my arm.

"What?" I asked.

"Be careful."

I grinned. "You be careful who you point that gun at."

The sirens were drawing closer.

Afterwards I couldn't recall crossing the road and unlocking the door. Six or seven long seconds I chose not to remember.

I'd started the engine and had the passenger door open for Candy before she reached the car. She was out of breath.

No sooner had she climbed in than the first police car squealed to a halt at the hotel entrance.

I waited for three uniformed men to disappear inside,

then engaged gear and eased the BMW slowly away from the kerb.

"How much money have you got?" I said.

"Quite a lot."

"What's it in?"

"Traveller's cheques mostly. Why?"

I swore. "You'll have to change it somewhere."

As fast as I dared, I started threading the BMW through the afternoon traffic on the road back to Duisburg again. This time I didn't forget the way.

"Where are we going?" she asked.

"My hotel. I need my passport. You've got yours, I hope? We'll have to get out of Germany."

She patted her bag. "I suppose I ought to say thank you or something—for rescuing me, I mean. If I wasn't so weak and shaky, I don't think I'd believe it really happened."

"I hate to tell you," I said, "it's not over and we're in big trouble. Thanks for the thought, though." I smiled at her. "I've never rescued anyone before. Not like that, anyway."

"We'll have to find a hospital," she said seriously. "Your face needs stitching—it looks dreadful."

"It's okay—it'll have to be. We've got to lose ourselves fast. The police probably have our descriptions by now and they'll certainly have found the mess on your bedroom floor. Your name was on the hotel register and I was seen on the way to your room, so we haven't got long. I just hope it takes a while to trace where I've been staying."

"We could go to the U.S. consul in Bonn," she said. "Or to the British embassy."

"Not now we can't. Can you imagine trying to explain this to anyone? We don't even understand what's going on ourselves."

"So what do we do?" Her expression changed. "You're not going to take off by yourself, are you? You won't, will you?"

"How do you think you'd make out?"

"Don't joke. Please."

"I'm not sure what we ought to do," I said. "All I have are a few ideas." I was surprised she thought I might walk out on her.

"What ideas?"

I squeezed the BMW past a slow-moving Mercedes and kept in the outside lane. "First we collect my passport and scrape together as much money as we can—in cash. Then I need to take a quick look at a crater."

"That's too dangerous," she said. "We daren't go back to the depot now. Rochling will have been told to look out for us. The police are there already, anyway."

"Not that crater. Another one. I never got around to telling you about it. The terrorists blew a water main a few minutes before they hit the tanks."

"Was that the first bang I heard?" she asked. "Over on the west side of the depot?"

"That was it. Luckily they chose the wrong pipeline."

"Why on earth do you want to see that crater?" There was a slight edge to her voice.

"To see how powerful the blast was," I lied. "It'll only take a minute."

She frowned but avoided pressing the point. "We still have to decide what we're going to do. We can't just go somewhere and hide. Sooner or later we'll have to clear things with the German police."

I glanced sideways at her. "We're not a couple of tourists who've got a parking ticket. There's a dead man back in your hotel room, Candy. There are also bullet holes in the walls, four video tapes and the equipment I hired to play them on. I can't make much sense out of all that and I can promise you the German police won't either. There are a few things to sort out before we can even think of talking to anyone."

"But you will help me?"

"For Christ's sake. The police and two rabid killers are after us. We're going to help each other. We're in this way over our heads and we're in it together."

"Because of me," she said slowly. "It's my fault, isn't it?"

"Right. You've got a lot of explaining to do, Candy Stafford."

"There's not much more to explain. You do believe these are the same people that murdered my father, though, don't you? You believe what I told you now?"

I nodded. "I believe you. I don't pretend to understand what it's all about but I believe you."

"So why look at the crater?" She asked the question without looking at me.

It hurt my cheek but I couldn't stop a grin. "In case I can learn something from it."

Suddenly she leaned across and kissed me.

"You saved my life. I don't think I can handle that—not after what's happened. I've never met anyone like you before."

"Maybe you're lucky. And don't start telling me I can subtract one from the twenty-eight lives you think I'm carrying around on my shoulders. You've got that wrong."

"There you go again. It's your chip, not mine. Stop pretending to be someone you're not—stop pretending you don't care about anything."

"You don't know the first damn thing about me, Candy. People who work with bombs spend half their lives being frightened. In the end you either go to pieces or you get so you don't care much at all."

"I don't believe you. You care all right. You want not to, but you do."

I smiled at her. "This is a hell of a time for psychoanalysis. How about laying off me and figuring out a survival plan for the next few days instead?"

"All right." She pointed. "We're nearly into Duisburg, aren't we?"

"We'll be back at the hotel in a couple of minutes," I said. "When we get there I'll use one of the back doors. You stay in the car. As soon as I get back we'll find somewhere to change your traveller's cheques and then go and look at the crater—after that we ought to dump the car. There may be an alert out on it already."

It was four o'clock when I stopped the BMW in the small gravelled car park at the rear of the hotel. I left the engine running and told Candy to sit behind the wheel. "If I'm more than five minutes, get the hell out of it," I said. "I mean what I say."

She took a tissue from her bag. "Spit on this," she said. "Let me wipe some of the blood off your face. You look awful." She was trying not to appear nervous.

I didn't take the tissue. "There isn't time. I'll have a quick rinse when I get upstairs. Don't let anyone see you waiting if you can help it."

Once inside the hotel I used the stairs instead of the elevator and reached the landing to the second floor without meeting anyone. At the door to my room I paused. If the police were here they'd have made their move before now—but that didn't mean it was safe to go in. Recent experience had made me wary of German hotel rooms.

Standing well to one side of the door I unlocked it and kicked it open. I wished I hadn't left the gun in the car.

By the time I'd decided there were no unpleasant surprises waiting for me, my heart was banging and my system had gone into overload again.

The room had been made up. The TV aerial had been fixed and the bowl on the table had been refilled with fruit. After I'd locked the door behind me I checked that my passport was still in my case and went to the bathroom mirror.

My face was a mess. Even after I'd washed the blood away it didn't look much better and the split in my cheek was a good deal uglier than it felt.

Later I'd have to figure out some way of fixing it but for the moment repairs were out of the question.

I stuffed a box of Band-Aid in my pocket, checked the contents of my case again and left immediately.

Thirty seconds later when I rejoined Candy in the BMW I saw she was holding the gun in her lap. She wriggled over to let me in.

"What's the matter?" I said quickly.

"I'm not sure," she said.

"Never mind whether you're sure or not, tell me."

"You know those photos I took. They'd been delivered to the hotel while I was out. I've just looked at them—I didn't have a chance before."

"And?"

"Two of them show the Rochling gate with the fire burning in the background. They're not good shots but clear enough to pick out cars and things. In both pictures there's a white Volkswagen van parked about a hundred yards away." She hesitated before going on. "There was a white VW van outside my hotel when you dropped me there—remember?"

"There are twenty-six million VW Kombis in Germany, Candy."

She nodded. "I know. But I just saw another one. While I was waiting for you. It was going slowly along there." She pointed at the entrance to the car park. "The same kind with windows in the sides. I thought it might be the same one."

Too much had happened to dismiss it as a coincidence and I was in no frame of mind to take chances.

"Did the driver see you?" I asked.

"I don't know. He could have."

"Seat belt," I instructed, "and keep your head down

when we hit the street." I released the hand brake and buckled my own belt.

"You don't really think they're waiting outside, do you?" she asked slowly. "Not here in the open."

"They knew which hotel you were staying at in Krefeld and I've got a nasty feeling they know I was staying at this one. If it's the same van, it'll be outside all right. Are you ready?"

She forced a smile. "You keep asking me that. I wasn't ready for any of this."

I wasn't either but I didn't say so. Instead, I lined the BMW with the gate, tramped down on the accelerator and dropped the clutch.

We came off the gravel sideways with the engine howling and hit the tarmac much too fast. I caught a second slide in time to avoid the concrete post—then we were out in the street. The hapless driver of a Citroën saw the BMW coming and saved both of us by swerving into the side of a parked car. Simultaneously the windshield exploded in my face.

I'd turned the wrong way. Flashes of light stabbed out at us from a white van and more of the BMW's windows shattered.

In front of me a bullet glanced off the steering-column but at this speed we were a difficult target and provided our luck held we had an even chance of getting away with it. Keeping my foot down I started weaving in and out of the traffic.

"Are you okay?" I yelled at Candy.

She surfaced from the floor with her hair all over her face. "I think so," she shouted.

I changed into third, giving the BMW its head for another few hundred yards before I slowed down.

"We made it," Candy breathed. "But you're mad. Out of your mind."

"We're alive," I said. "Don't forget that."

Strangely, this time I hadn't been afraid and the sick, weak feeling I'd experienced earlier seemed to have disappeared. An imagined superiority of the BMW over a Volkswagen van perhaps, or maybe because I'd had some control over the situation and had an idea of what we could expect.

"We'll have to dump the car somewhere," I said. "God knows how many people saw us back there."

"We've still got to change my traveller's cheques," Candy said, "and you want to see that other crater, don't you?"

"We're on the way to the crater now," I said. "At least I hope we are. It'll be dark soon and I'm not sure where it is."

"Look," she said. "I know we've just been shot at again and I know this is the wrong time, but there's something I have to talk to you about. You're not going to like it but it can't wait."

"Christ," I said. "That's all I need. I suppose it's something you've forgotten to mention until now."

"No, it isn't. Do you want to hear it or not? It's important."

It was freezing inside the BMW. With no windshield and two other windows missing, even at 30 mph there was a gale blowing round my ears and my face was stinging from the cold.

"I need a drink," I said.

She looked annoyed. "Don't you want to know what I have to say?"

"No. But I'd better hear it. It can't make anything worse."

"You know the man you shot—the one with the scar—you saw me take his wallet on the way out."

I didn't say anything.

"While you were getting your passport I went through it. There was a driver's licence, business cards, some cash and two credit cards—company ones. Are you listening?"

"Yes, but I've got to figure out where I'm going at the same time. Go on."

"His name was Barak Pang and he worked for a company called China Construction. I'm sure I remember seeing that in my father's notes somewhere. I don't think he knew where the company was based, though—at least I don't think he did."

"Where is it based?" I asked.

"Hong Kong."

I turned the car down a side street that would take us close to the Rochling depot. By following the perimeter fence until it met the Rhine, I hoped to cross the Bergedorfer Strasse near the spot where Keller said the terrorists had destroyed the water main.

More by accident than design we seemed to have uncovered a good deal of information about the organisation that was trying to keep us quiet. There was absolutely no doubt that the van in Candy's photos was connected with the Rochling fire and if she was telling the truth—if her father really had learned of the China Construction Company months ago—why couldn't I put it all together so it made sense?

"What's the important bit?" I said.

"I know this is the craziest thing you've heard but I think we should go to Hong Kong. I've got enough money for the fares. We can change my traveller's cheques at the air terminal."

"Why the bloody hell should I go to Hong Kong?"

"Because you said you believed me and because I need you to help me. I've already explained all that to you. There isn't anyone else and you're part of this whole thing now. You're as involved as I am."

Outrageous though it was, the suggestion had a degree of logic to it. Warped logic perhaps, but I had killed someone, men with guns were after us and I was far from confident of talking my way out if and when we ran foul of the police.

Rounding a bend to see a signpost marked BERGEDORFER STRASSE but travelling too fast to stop, I braked heavily and reversed back to the intersection.

I didn't speak until we were moving again. "I hadn't planned on a trip to Hong Kong, Candy."

"Had you planned on the Rochling fire? Did you plan on getting mixed up with me?"

"No," I snapped. "Shut up for a minute, will you, I think that's the place." I pointed to a group of oildrums surrounding what looked like a hole in the road.

I parked the BMW ten feet from the drums and got out. "Don't go away," I said.

The road was surfaced with best-quality German tarmac and I was relieved to see the crater hadn't been filled in yet.

It was about ten feet in diameter and roughly circular. All around it the roadside was smeared with mud but the edges of the hole told me what I wanted to know. Unlike the brittle concrete at the Rochling tank farm, the softer tarmac of the Bergedorfer Strasse revealed everything. Deep below the ground a giant bubble had burst, curling the crater edges as it smashed upwards through the surface. An unmistakable sign that the blast had originated underneath the tarmac and not from a charge placed on top of it.

I returned to the car, climbing in and slamming the door hard. Events were overtaking me and my thought process seemed incapable of explaining the incredible muddle I found myself in. I needed to think, time to put some of the pieces of this jigsaw together. But time was something we were running out of fast.

"It was an underground explosion, wasn't it?" Candy said.

I nodded.

"We can't stay in Germany, Paul," she said gently. "Either those men will kill us or we'll get caught."

"I know. That doesn't mean going to Hong Kong is a good idea."

"We have to find out what all this means—carry on where my father left off. It's a way to get ourselves out of this dreadful mess—maybe the only way. I'm sorry I've dragged you into it but I can't undo it now."

If we were going to leave Germany, we didn't have long to do it in. Already the police might have sealed off the air terminal and with my cheek split open I was easily recognisable wherever I went.

Candy took one of my hands in hers. "I promise to do whatever you want—whatever you say—but please let's go to Hong Kong. We must be able to get some sort of lead there—if we work together—help each other like you said."

"Don't push too hard," I warned. "I might think of another way out—or is that what you're scared of?"

"I'm scared, period. I'm especially scared you might decide to do something by yourself—without me."

"Have you been to Hong Kong before?" I asked her.

"No. Have you?"

"Once."

She stared directly at me. "Please, Paul."

"You're right," I said slowly. "It's the craziest thing I've ever heard."

But four and a half hours later, with a fresh bandage on my face and with an unknown future ahead of me, I felt more alive than I had done for years. I leaned back in my seat as flight LH 661 for Karachi and Hong Kong left the runway and climbed steeply into a star-filled night.

SEVEN

A long international flight provides an exceptional opportunity for thinking. Hour after uninterrupted hour to sit and sift through the jumble of half-related facts and events that somehow I had to piece together.

Under Candy's disapproving eye I spent the first hour unwinding. Lufthansa run a civilised airline and buy their scotch from one of the best distilleries in Scotland.

Not until dinner was over was I ready to attempt an analysis of everything that had happened to us. We ordered more coffee then started at the beginning by reviewing what Candy had learned from her father's notes. But thirty minutes later she was asleep with her head resting on my shoulder. Both of us were weary and, even though she'd fought against it, the combination of strain and shock had finally caught up with her.

I tucked a blanket round her, closed my eyes too and let the whisky do its work.

We woke up together at the end of the movie. The cabin lights had come on and people were scrambling for the toilet.

"Have you been asleep?" Candy asked.

"No," I lied. "Thought I ought to stand guard."

"Tell me about the movie then." She laughed.

"I didn't watch. I've been thinking."

"Let me have a look at your bandage." I felt her fingers on my cheek.

Before we'd checked in, Candy had pulled my face together with what she called "butterflies"—narrow strips of adhesive plaster twisted in their centre and stuck across the split in my cheek. Afterwards, for cosmetic reasons, she'd covered the butterflies with a dressing which also served to conceal the worst of the bruising.

"It's stopped bleeding," she said. "How does it feel?"

"Okay, now you've stopped poking it around."

"You'll have an awful scar. Do you mind?"

I grinned at her. "No, I don't mind. I'm just pleased I'm not full of bullet holes. Someone must have been looking out for us."

"Eventually the German police are bound to discover we caught this flight," she said. "They'll know we had tickets to Hong Kong. Won't that mean they'll ask the Hong Kong police to find us?"

"They'll ask," I said. "But the Hong Kong police have plenty on their hands without bothering about you and me. Anyway, it's impossible to find anyone in Hong Kong. It's the best place in the world to get lost in. That's not the problem. If you want to worry about something, figure out how long our cash is going to last."

"We've still got over two thousand Deutschmarks. I can send to the States for more money if it isn't too dangerous to do that."

"Let's see how we get on first," I said. "You're the nearest —what about getting some coffee from the galley? Then, so long as you can keep awake, we'll exchange theories and decide what we're going to do."

"All right. I'll only be a minute."

Earlier in the flight I'd learned little new about her father's investigation. His notes had been stolen before Candy had been able to copy them and all she'd managed to save were a few photographs Desmond Stafford had collected in the course of his travels. She'd brought them to Germany with her, hoping I might be interested, but they were thousands of miles behind us now, somewhere in Candy's bloodstained hotel room. The envelope she'd brought to my hotel the morning after the fire had contained a few photographs and a letter he'd written to her shortly before his death. Although Candy said some of the photos showed the Stockton tank farm that had been destroyed, it didn't sound as though they'd add much to what we already knew but I would have liked to read the letter, if only out of curiosity.

Candy returned carrying two plastic cups. I held them for her while she sat down. "Okay," she said, "you can start. I'm ready for theory number one."

"I've only got one."

She sipped her coffee. "That's one more than I have. I promise I won't go to sleep again."

"All right. How about this? Before he died your father had convinced himself that these fires were all started by underground bomb blasts. He was absolutely sure, wasn't he?"

She nodded.

"Well, I think he was right. The crater I saw at the Rochling depot looked like half of it was underneath the bottom rim of the tank. It didn't register at the time but that was probably because I never considered the explosion could have originated below ground. I suppose I'd persuaded myself a surface charge could have done the same sort of damage, but now I think back I don't think it could. Anyway, anyone who knew what they were looking for could see it was an underground explosion that carved out the hole in the Bergedorfer Strasse. So, on the basis of two craters I've seen, I've decided to go along with your father's idea."

"That's not a new theory, though," Candy said. "It's not even yours, it was my father's."

"I know. I haven't finished. The idea of underground

explosions doesn't make sense unless you've got an explanation for them—a way to explain how the bombs got there in the first place. Terrorists don't go around with concrete-cutters and pneumatic drills where everyone can see them. My theory takes over where your father's left off." I paused. "I think we're dealing with a remote-controlled tunnelling device."

Candy raised her eyebrows. "A special machine, you mean?"

"Right. Special, small and very clever. Something about a foot in diameter capable of worming its way for long distances through the subsoil. It wouldn't be difficult to design a digging head to do the job. All you'd need is a good, powerful hydraulic motor and some form of radio-controlled guidance system. The biggest problem would be feeding power to it but I think the head could be made to drag hydraulic lines and an electric cable along behind it."

"A mole," Candy exclaimed. "A mechanical mole. Would a thing like that really work?"

"Yes, I think so. It'd cost a hell of a lot to build and I don't know what sort of distances it could be made to travel over but the technology isn't too way out."

"But if it cost a lot, the owners wouldn't want to blow it up, would they?"

"They wouldn't have to. Imagine it's an underground missile with a nose cone full of high explosive. When it reaches wherever it's been told to go, someone pushes a button to detach the warhead, then pulls the digging head out on the end of its control lines—or makes it reverse out by itself. Then two hours or two days later a timer triggers a detonator in the warhead. The operator doesn't need to be anywhere near it. Once the mole's burrowed its way to the target and dumped its charge, all you have to do is reel it in, pack up and disappear—climb on a plane back to Hong Kong, maybe."

"You're not making fun of me, are you?" she said.

"No," I laughed. "I'm perfectly serious. All it would take is a couple of good engineers and a heap of money."

"Then that's it. That's how they do it. My God, what an incredible idea."

"Hey," I said. "Hold on a minute. My theory only explains bits of what you and I know about."

"But the mole explains everything—don't be so modest."

I was amused by her enthusiasm. She was beginning to unwind and, for the first time since I'd met her, she stopped searching for ways to convince me to help her. Candy and I had known each other for a very short while indeed but the bizarre events which had drawn us together were having an effect. Growing between us was something that went beyond the need to help each other. A bond I was far from ready to accept despite an unwillingness to reject it. Not only had my reservations about her vanished but I could detect a sense of freedom I hadn't experienced for years—a feeling of having escaped from myself or from a self-made trap.

"What's the matter?" she enquired.

"Nothing."

"You're not thinking backwards again, are you—not over what's been before?"

"The last few days, you mean?"

She shook her head. "The last few years."

I smiled. "You're a perceptive young lady but I wish you'd get off my back."

"Sorry. I thought I noticed something different about you."

"Good, bad or just different?"

"Good. Look at me a minute."

I crushed my empty cup and met her eyes. "I'm not sitting here because I want to," I said. "Remember?"

"I remember." She looked away. "What's so wrong about your mole idea?"

Her attempt to change the subject had been as abrupt as it had been clumsy but I was still unwilling to draw conclusions. "The mole idea's all right," I said, "provided you only connect China Construction with what happened at the tank farm in Duisburg. Try and extend underground burrowing any further than that and the whole thing falls apart."

"No it doesn't," she replied. "Suppose the China Construction Company really has built a machine just like the one you described. They could have used it anywhere, anywhere they wanted."

"Sure they could but what the hell for? Why travel round the world digging holes and hiding bombs in them?"

"Oh." She frowned. "Maybe the China Construction Company is run by the Communists. It's based in Hong Kong, so it could be."

I thought for a moment. "A bunch of German terrorists are the last people Communist China would want to get mixed up with. Why would the Chinese set fire to the Stockton tank farm where your father worked? That was a Soviet operation and the Red Chinese are less friendly with the Russians than they are with the Americans. Anyway, what could the Chinese hope to gain by blowing up air terminal buildings and the other things your father discovered?"

"I don't know." She stared at her lap. "Nothing, I guess."

I wished there was something I could say to revive her enthusiasm. The mole idea had grown on me as I'd described it to her, but we needed motives, not science fiction tools which could put explosive charges in place. A motive to explain why a Hong Kong construction company should travel round the world destroying oil depots and buildings apparently at random. Even if I could think of an explanation, linking it to such unlikely organisations as the German Red Army and the Soviet KGB presented a major problem.

The men who'd tried to kill us in Germany had been convinced our very existence posed a threat to them. Yet try as I might, I could think of nothing we knew and nothing we'd done that would make us dangerous to anyone. We were as ignorant of their business as Candy's father had been. Or, before he'd been murdered, had he stumbled upon something that we hadn't?

I straightened my legs, wedging them under the seat in front of me while I stretched. A long haul in a 747 might give time to think but I hadn't yet found an airline that designed seats for people like me.

Candy sensed my discomfort. "I don't mind if you walk around for a while," she said. "I'll stand guard here." She smiled. "Go on. You've been sitting down too long."

I climbed out to the aisle, my imagination stirring slightly as my arm brushed against her. I dismissed the thought. The memory of Lisa was too close to the surface and in our present circumstances ideas like that were madness.

Pretending there was a good reason why I should be on a flight from Germany to Hong Kong, I walked slowly to the rear of the aircraft between rows of sleeping passengers. But the illusion of freedom persisted and if Lisa hadn't drifted into my thoughts I could have persuaded myself that things really had changed.

I used a toilet in the tail, then made my way back up the opposite aisle until I reached the forward galley.

Outside it two flight attendants were sitting shoeless on fold-down seats. One of them stood up and started to look efficient.

"It's okay," I said. "All I need are two miniature bottles of scotch. I know where to find the water and the ice."

She handed them to me. "I hope they help. What happened?" She pointed at my bandage.

"Car accident," I said. "Thanks."

After I'd emptied one of the bottles into a paper cup and added a couple of ice cubes I went to stand by the emergency hatch where there was more room. I wondered what Geoff Green was doing and whether the Duisburg police had interviewed Keller yet.

It took half an hour for the scotch to work again and I was on the point of returning to my seat when Candy appeared beside me.

"What are you doing?" she asked quietly.

"Not a hell of a lot."

"I got lonely."

"Planes are lonely places," I said. "You can get more lonely in a plane along with three hundred other people than you can in a car by yourself."

She nodded but didn't say anything. The light from the galley threw a shadow across her face but I could tell something was wrong.

"What is it, Candy," I asked.

She didn't answer.

"Candy," I said gently. "You're not alone."

She came to me and buried her head in my shoulder while she cried.

The whisky, the roar of the jet and the girl in my arms—a soft-focus dream of two other people—two strangers who, just like us, needed time to catch their breath and decide where they were heading.

It was nearly one in the morning when the 747 touched down in the narrow strip of land which is Hong Kong's Kai Tak airport. No one arrested us as we disembarked and the immigration man who stamped our passports was tired and uninterested. I told him we were on holiday, travelling on to Tokyo in a few days' time.

Downstairs in the baggage claim area I took Candy's arm

and made for the nearest counter where a Chinese customs officer was waiting for customers. I needed to explain our lack of suitcases.

"Can you tell me who to contact about lost luggage, please?" I asked. "We were on flight 661 but our cases didn't come off a connecting flight from London in time."

"If you telephone in the morning the Lufthansa office will let you know when the next flight from Germany arrives." He pointed at Candy's handbag. "May I see, please?"

Before leaving Germany we'd thrown the gun into the Rhine and the bag contained nothing unusual but Candy was plainly nervous.

He gave it back after a perfunctory inspection and said we could go.

"Come on," I said. "We're first out. Let's get a taxi before the rush starts."

"Why did he go through my bag?" she asked when we were outside.

"Because he didn't have anything else to look at. Don't worry about it—we've arrived. Welcome to Hong Kong."

After the cold of Duisburg, just to stand in Hong Kong's moist, warm air was almost sensuous. Even in the loading zone outside the terminal, exhaust fumes couldn't mask the distinctive smell of the most densely populated city in the world. It was a long time since I'd been here but Hong Kong was a place no one ever forgot. A place Candy and I were going to share with five million Chinese while we tried to solve the puzzle that had brought us all this way.

I waved down a taxi and held the door while she got in.

"Hotel Miramar," I told the driver.

The streets weren't too crowded but when we pulled up at the entrance to the hotel her expression was one of astonishment.

"Wow," she said. "I never expected it to be like this."

"Don't forget it's the middle of the night," I said. "If you think this is busy, wait until tomorrow morning. Stay here a second while I go in and change some Deutschmarks so we can pay the taxi fare."

I returned to find her talking busily to the driver. He had his finger on the street map, giving directions to the Peking Road—the address of the China Construction Company.

"Slow down," I said. "Stop being so eager." I gave the driver a fifty-dollar note and pulled her out onto the pavement.

She skipped along beside me into the foyer.

"Mr. and Mrs. Gregory," I said. "James and Anne from 12, Woodbridge Road, Winchester, England. Can you remember that?"

She nodded. "Will they want our passport numbers?"

"Yes. Pretend to check but don't put down the real one. Don't do anything obvious like reversing the numbers, either."

We registered together at the counter while Candy explained how our luggage had failed to come off the British Airways flight this afternoon. She was disturbingly good at it.

A few minutes later she was bouncing up and down on one of the Miramar's expensive beds with a huge grin on her face.

"James Gregory," she laughed. "You're a very special person—did anyone ever tell you that?"

"Not lately."

She teetered on the edge of the mattress, making me catch her as she toppled forwards. Suddenly her mood changed.

"What do you say to someone who's saved your life, put you on a plane and carried you off to Hong Kong?" she asked quietly.

My arms were round her but I was searching for Lisa in her eyes.

"Did you love her very dearly?" she whispered.

"Does it show that much?"

She smiled. "It was you who said I was perceptive. I'm good at guessing. I think I'd like you to kiss me now."

Her breath was warm against my face as she leaned forwards.

"You're crazy," I said softly.

"I can make you forget." She kissed me with her eyes wide open. "I promise you I can."

It was too easy to believe she could take the hurt away but when our lips met again I found I could believe anything at all.

EIGHT

I woke up gradually, uncertain of my ability to distinguish
dream from reality. But the sunlight pouring through the
windows was real enough—so was the girl asleep beside me
on the bed. Everything was real. The sky on fire above the
Rochling depot, a night flight from Germany to Hong Kong
and someone called Candy Stafford—not the tangled elements of a dream as they should have been but a series of
interwoven events that had really happened.

Needing to be certain, I placed a hand gently on Candy's
shoulder.

She turned over reaching out for me without opening her
eyes. I pulled her hair away from her face.

"Hi," I said.

"What time is it?" she asked.

"Nine-thirty. Are you going to wake up or not?"

"Not yet. You might not really be there. I don't want to
spoil it."

"Suppose I'm not who you think I am?" I said.

She opened an eye. "Paul Harwood," she said. "Known
sometimes as James Gregory, explosives expert, unmarried.
Born in Wiltshire, England, 1949. Is that you?"

"Scar on the left cheek," I said, "temporarily disguised
with sticking plaster."

"Okay. You pass." She laughed happily. "That means I
ought to be in Hong Kong. I'd better check that out, too."

"Have a look outside."

"I haven't got any clothes on."

"I know," I said.

She wrapped herself ineffectually in the bedspread and padded over to the window and stood with her back to me. "What do we do first?" she asked.

"Eat."

"Then what?" She swung round. "We need to buy clothes and things. We haven't even got toothbrushes. I suppose we should do that first."

"Not before breakfast," I said. "Here." I threw her clothes at her. Grabbing at them she succeeded in tripping over the bedspread and wound up on the floor.

"China Construction, here we come," I laughed. "I hope they're ready for us."

She stood up and disappeared into the shower leaving me to decide whether there was some way the China Construction Company could have learned of our presence in Hong Kong.

By the time we'd finished breakfast I'd thought about it long enough. The Chinese who'd tried to kill us in Germany might have guessed we'd search the wallet of their colleague but they'd hardly expect us to go to Hong Kong. Even if they could think of a reason why we should do such a thing, we'd travelled here so quickly that surprise was on our side.

We had two choices. Carry on moving rapidly in an attempt to find the answers we needed or, in view of last night, forget the whole damn thing and concentrate instead on what was happening between us.

I stopped Candy as she began to leave the table. "There's something we haven't talked about yet," I said.

"You and me," she replied. "You want to talk about last night, don't you?"

"Don't you think it's a good idea?"

"Why not ask me if I make a habit of sleeping with men who save my life?" Her mouth was a tight line. "That's what you want to know, isn't it?"

"No. Stop trying to be smart."

"What then?"

"I want to know if last night opens up any new options."

She coloured slightly. "Did it occur to you I might feel the same way?"

I nodded. "I figure we should talk things through. We're wanted for murder in Germany and it'd be tough to dig ourselves out of the hole when we haven't got the answers yet, but that doesn't mean we have to go ahead with all this. We can stop right now. There are plenty of places where we could lose ourselves for as long as we like—forever, if it works out."

"Disappear, you mean?" Her anger had evaporated.

"We've half disappeared already," I said.

"Do you think you've known me long enough to make that sort of proposition?" There was a suggestion of a smile on her lips now.

"No." I grinned. "I take my chances when they turn up. Story of my life."

"We could do both, couldn't we?" she said. "Do what we came here to do—tell the story to a newspaper maybe— then disappear—just you and me on a plane to nowhere."

I studied her face wondering what had sparked off the magic and how it could have come so very quickly.

"Paul," she said quietly, "if it's what you want, I'll go with you—now—wherever you say—that is what you're asking me, isn't it?"

I hadn't expected plain acceptance. Neither had I expected the feelings inside me that came with her answer. No one had said such a thing to me before. Once, at the beginning, I thought Lisa might have done but an overseas assignment had somehow interfered and afterwards the commitment hadn't been there.

I continued staring at her, struggling for the right words.

"Paul?" she queried.

"Perhaps we could do both," I said. "Let's have a look at the Peking Road first. We can do our shopping as we go."

She followed me from the breakfast room but pulled me to one side outside the door.

"You know what you said about taking chances?" she whispered. "I don't think there are any." She stood on tiptoe and kissed me gently on the mouth.

We arrived in the Peking Road at the wrong time. A truck and a taxi were locked in combat on top of a traffic island and the whole street was so choked with cars, taxis and pedestrians that it was almost impassable.

Candy strengthened her grip on my arm. "I'd never find the hotel again," she said. "Not without melting, anyway. Don't lose me, will you."

It was less than a fifteen-minute walk back to the Miramar but I knew how she felt. Despite the summer-weight clothes we'd bought, twice on the way here we'd been forced to take refuge in an air-conditioned store and the need for another jolt of cool air was increasing by the minute.

A nearby electronics shop looked promising, but no sooner had we reached it than Candy pointed.

And there, on the opposite side of the street, were the registered offices of the China Construction Company—or at least a sign saying that's what they were. Air-conditioning units protruded from each of the upstairs windows and although in Hong Kong air conditioning itself wasn't a sign of excessive affluence, the building was obviously one of the more expensive in the block. Each side of the front door enormous colour photos prevented anyone from seeing through the street-level windows. The pictures of a large suspension bridge and an offshore oil rig seemed appropriate. I wondered if they represented China Construction's past successes or whether the bridge and oil rig were scheduled for accidents in the future.

"What now?" Candy asked.

"Come back after closing time. See if there's a back door somewhere—off another street, perhaps. The Hyatt Regency's back on the corner—how about having a quiet drink there while we look at the map?"

She nodded. "Anywhere. Just as long as it's cool."

Besides being cool, the downstairs bar in the Hyatt had two fountains, a waterfall and plenty of empty tables. After the noise of the street outside it was also very quiet.

I ordered a Campari and orange juice for each of us—a drink designed especially for hot mornings in Hong Kong.

"Not scotch?" Candy asked.

"I want to think. Scotch is to help you stop thinking."

"Oh," she said. "You must have needed a lot of help on the plane."

"That was last night or last week—I can't remember."

She raised her eyebrows. "It certainly works, doesn't it."

I grinned. "Not entirely. Some of last night I remember very clearly."

"The map," she said firmly. "The map." She unfolded it and spread it on the table.

The offices of China Construction were not well placed at all. According to the map the building could be reached only from the Peking Road and to complicate matters the Central Post Office wasn't far away, nor was the Kowloon Police Station.

"There isn't another way in," I said.

"What about windows round the back?" Candy swivelled the map round and inspected it more closely.

I shook my head. "I don't think so. The offices only occupy part of the building. We might be able to break in somewhere through a side door or a window but that doesn't necessarily get us into China Construction. I was hoping for one of those tacky plywood places you find in the back streets."

"Okay—so we use the front door," Candy said. "All we have to do is figure out how."

"We can hardly break in straight through the front door," I said. "The street'll be crawling with people all night. Half Hong Kong works in the day and the other half works at night. Assuming we don't want to walk in during working hours, there's only one way and that's with a key."

Candy smiled at me. "So we need a Harwood plan. You're working on it already."

"What makes you say that?"

"You're frowning—sort of. I've seen you do it before."

"I'm frowning because I think we're being stupid." I made an effort to alter my expression. "We don't even know what we're looking for once we get inside."

"A mole," she said brightly. "Your mechanical mole."

"Covered in instantly recognisable Duisburg soil," I said. "Parked in the basement somewhere."

"I'm serious. You don't know what we might find in there." Candy looked at me over the rim of her glass. "It'd be stupid to come all this way and not even try, wouldn't it?"

"Your lack of subtlety is showing," I said.

She feigned astonishment. "I was just saying how I feel about things."

"Okay," I said. "How about this?" I started speaking before I'd formulated my ideas properly, but Candy's enthusiasm was infectious and it wasn't long before we had a plan that I thought offered at least some chances of success. Although by no means an ambitious plan, it had the virtue of simplicity and exposed us to minimum risk in the event of failure. With time on our side the risk factor was important, and, as I tried to explain, provided we weren't arrested on our first attempt we could always try again.

To begin with, Candy was unhappy about waiting until evening before we made our move but soon we were talking about ourselves and for the next few hours we managed to forget everything except each other. We stayed at the Hyatt for lunch and left holding hands like a pair of teenagers.

The remainder of the day was spent in keeping cool and making preparations—activities which proved equally difficult and took roughly the same amount of time.

Eventually, at four-thirty in the afternoon, we were back in the Hyatt bar with our equipment—two paper bags, two toy guns and a camera. To guard against any slip in confidence, on this occasion I'd ordered something stronger than Campari and orange juice.

"You haven't got a vivid imagination, have you?" I said to Candy.

"Why?"

"I hoped you weren't wondering what the inside of a Hong Kong jail looks like."

"Are you trying to put me off?"

"Damn you. I feel all crawly now. Maybe it'll be better if your idea doesn't work."

I inspected my watch. "Let's go and see. Time we were off."

"I'm scared," she said. "Why did I talk you out of disappearing?" She smiled as she stood up. "I've never done anything like this, Paul. I mightn't be any good at it."

"You'll be all right," I promised. "This is hardly in the same league as our German operations."

The afternoon was nearly over but it was still hot outside and, if anything, there were more people and more cars in the Peking Road than there had been earlier in the day.

Three minutes after we'd left the bar we were waiting on the far side of the street observing the offices we'd come to burgle. We didn't have long to wait. At one minute to five o'clock the door opened and a smartly dressed Chinese gentleman stepped out. A customer perhaps—or one of China Construction's employees leaving early?

I held up a finger to Candy who was standing fifty feet

away on a traffic island. She nodded and pointed across the street where another man had emerged from the building. I had only the briefest glimpse of him before a passing truck blocked my view. When I could see again he'd vanished into the crowd.

Apart from trucks and the odd bus which got in the way, from where we stood Candy and I were unlikely to miss anyone leaving the front door of China Construction. We were well positioned and had an advantage over the average Hong Kong pedestrian simply because we were a lot taller. Even so, as a precaution, I'd stationed Candy some distance down the street on the traffic island.

By quarter past five a woman and three more men had left the building. So far none of them had given me the clue I was looking for and I was almost on the point of deciding no one else was going to appear when the door opened again. The man who came out this time was indistinguishable from his predecessors but his pattern of behaviour differed from the others'. Instead of walking away directly he paused to check that the door was locked behind him.

I'd been hoping to see someone lock up from the outside but this would do. If I was right, the offices of the China Construction Company were now completely empty.

I signalled to Candy, then started off across the road. Unless I was quick, my target would vanish into the crowd like the others and the chance would be wasted.

By crossing the Peking Road diagonally I gained on him and soon I was close enough behind to recognise him if he got too far ahead. He walked as briskly as conditions allowed, stepping into the gutter when the sidewalk became too congested or holding his briefcase in front of him to force a path through the people.

My opportunity came unexpectedly when he stopped to inspect a display of international exchange rates in the window of a bank.

Standing close beside him I tapped him gently on the shoulder.

"I have a message for you," I said. "From a Mr. Barak Pang."

At the mention of Pang's name he turned to face me but made no attempt to move away. I fancied he was startled.

"It's in this paper bag," I said. Opening the top I allowed him to see the gun I was holding inside.

I carried on before he could say anything. "Unless you want to wind up as a nasty mess on the sidewalk, do exactly what I tell you," I said quietly. "You're going to walk back to your office and unlock the front door. I'll be right behind you."

"Who are you?" He spoke nervously and his left eye was twitching.

"I'll tell you when we're inside. Get moving."

He turned hesitantly and started retracing his steps. I saw Candy ahead of us. Once she saw me nod she, too, began making her way back to the office.

This was the critical part of the operation especially if he decided to yell. Although I'd dumped the bag containing the plastic Luger and now had my fist inside an empty bag of the same size, I was a Caucasian, not a Hong Kong Chinese, and even armed with nothing but an empty bag I could be accused of almost anything if the local constabulary felt so inclined.

He paused at the door to the offices searching for keys in his jacket pocket.

"Gently," I said. "Move too fast and you're dead."

I didn't know whether China Construction had heard about Pang yet but the cooperation I was receiving seemed to indicate that the news might well have filtered through.

The door clicked open.

"Inside," I said. I poked him with the bag.

Candy was beside me now, apprehension written all over

her. The three of us walked in together—an effortless break-in that perhaps had gone too smoothly.

Candy slipped our replacement toy gun into my hand. "How about that?" she whispered. "We've done it."

The man who had let us in was waiting for instructions. "Okay," I said. "We'll talk in your office. Where is it?"

He pointed to a flight of carpeted stairs. "I do not wish to talk to you."

"We'll see," I said. "Go on up."

A small reception area at the top of the stairs contained a desk and two visitors' chairs. He went to a walnut-panelled door behind the desk, unlocked it and stood aside to let Candy go in.

I shook my head. "You first." I moved the gun slightly hoping he wouldn't notice I was concealing most of it with my hand.

Once inside the office he seemed to relax slightly—either because he was on familiar ground or because he'd led us into a trap. He was about forty and had unusually light-coloured eyes for a dark-skinned oriental.

"You must be Mr. Harwood," he said, "and Miss Stafford, of course. Welcome to Hong Kong."

"You've heard from Duisburg," I said. "Or Krefeld."

He nodded. "A telex last night. Although I was not told to expect your arrival here."

"You know about Pang?" Candy asked.

"Indeed I do, Miss Stafford. You are speaking of my brother. My dead brother. I understand he died from gun-shot wounds in your hotel."

The conversation was already out of hand and I was getting more uncomfortable by the second.

"Stand over there," I instructed, "and don't move unless I tell you to."

"I assume you wish to search the files, Mr. Harwood? To get the information you and Miss Stafford require?"

"Right. Give me the keys to your desk."

He held out a key ring. "The small silver one for the top drawer."

"Why the hell are you being so helpful?" I snapped.

"Would you prefer I made you use violence to get what you want?"

"Take the key," I said to Candy. "See what's in the desk."

"You will find three ledgers in the top left-hand drawer," he said.

Candy took them out. She was uneasy now and I could see her hands shaking as she opened the cover of the first one.

Because he'd already learned of his brother's death in Germany and knew who we were, it was possible he believed he was dealing with a pair of experienced assassins, but somehow I knew that wasn't the right explanation. His attitude was more one of smug caution than of fear. Something was dreadfully wrong.

"What are they?" I asked Candy.

"Everything my father thought was true." She glanced up at me. "Everything."

"What is?"

"Lists. Contracts." Her face was pale. "We should never have come here, Paul."

"May I offer you a drink?" The man spoke calmly. "Put the gun away, Mr. Harwood. I will tell you whatever it is you want to know."

"You can tell me what the hell's going on," I said. "Start with that."

"I should have thought someone of your intellect would have already guessed. Do you honestly believe I would lead you back here and allow you to discover the nature of CCC's business interests around the world?"

"What does he mean?" Candy asked nervously.

"Look outside the door, Miss Stafford. Look outside the door."

"Don't," I yelled.

But there was no need for anyone to look outside the door.

Two armed men entered the office. Men who, only two days ago in Germany, had failed by the narrowest of margins to kill us.

NINE

It was Germany over again. Through my own stupidity I'd delivered us into the hands of the men who had been hunting us in Europe.

I could still hear Candy's stifled scream and the way she'd called my name as the door swung open. As well as betraying her confidence in me, I'd betrayed the promise of our future together even before it had begun.

She was standing frozen behind the desk, her eyes wide with terror. I moved towards her.

"Harwood," the large man snapped. "Stay where you are. Throw down the gun."

I let the plastic Luger slip from my fingers. My stomach was in knots and I could feel myself sweating.

"Kick it over here."

I did as he said.

He inspected it where it lay, then splintered it under his heel. "Search them," he said. "Both of them. Make sure of Harwood."

Pang's brother stepped over to Candy and ran his hands over her body. Even when he lifted her skirt and slid a hand quickly between her legs, she made no attempt to stop him.

His search of me was equally thorough but he was more careful not to screen his colleagues' line of fire.

Both men were carrying a type of gun I hadn't seen before—cheap semiautomatics fitted with long silencers. A bullet from them or a painless job from a hypodermic needle? I already knew they had no wish to keep us alive and this time they'd be waiting for me to try something.

I fought to meet the eyes of the big man.

"We are both surprised I think, Mr. Harwood," he said. "I am astonished at your persistence, or is it Miss Stafford we can thank for renewing our acquaintance again so soon?"

"How did you know we were here?" Candy whispered. "Tell us who you are."

"My name is Huang Inada, Miss Stafford, I am the senior director of China Construction. This is Mr. Tadashi." He nodded at the smaller man beside him. "Mr. Tadashi is our operations manager. Mr. Pang has already introduced himself, I believe. He of course runs our office here in Hong Kong. The man Mr. Harwood killed in your hotel was Mr. Pang's brother." He smiled thinly. "Are there more questions you wish to ask?"

"You have not explained how simple it was to trap our visitors," Pang interrupted. "Allow me to show you, Miss Stafford."

He stepped over to a wall-mounted cocktail cabinet and opened a door to reveal a panel of switches and small lights. Some of the lights were glowing.

I'd guessed as much. The premises of the China Construction Company were protected by an infrared, or photoelectric, burglar alarm system. Pang would have set it before he left and by omitting to override the circuits on reentering the building he'd been sure his colleagues would know of our arrival. To have appeared so quickly Inada and Tadashi must have been somewhere in the office complex or in a neighbouring part of the building when the alarm sounded.

Not to have guessed CCC would take precautions to protect their base was bad enough, but by ignoring the warning signs Pang had given me I'd blundered into a trap that had been set for common burglars. My luck had gone sour again and the feeling of helplessness was overwhelming.

Pang was clinking bottles at the cocktail cabinet. He passed glasses to Inada and Tadashi.

"And what will you drink, Miss Stafford?" he asked. "And you, Mr. Harwood?"

"Nothing," I said.

Inada pulled up a chair and sat down. He'd put his gun away but Tadashi still carried his.

I was unprepared for Inada's next remark.

"Well, Mr. Harwood, I think some explanations are overdue. My colleagues and I will decide what to do with you after we've heard what you and Miss Stafford have to say."

Although the offer of a drink was contrived, the suggestion that we had something to talk about seemed to indicate Inada wasn't planning to kill us immediately. Why that should be remained to be seen but I doubted the reprieve would be for long.

"You travelled here directly from Germany?" Inada queried.

I nodded.

"But not before speaking to friends or taking some other steps to protect yourselves?"

Unwittingly, he had given himself away. Had Inada overestimated me as I had overestimated him?

I searched furiously for the bluff, the double bluff, then seized the only opportunity we might get.

"You don't imagine we'd come to Hong Kong and break in here without some kind of insurance, do you?" I said quietly.

"No. I don't believe you would, Mr. Harwood. That is precisely why you may present a problem to us. I don't suppose I can persuade you to reveal the nature of this insurance, as you call it?"

Did Inada genuinely believe we'd told someone what we

intended to do? Had he really fooled himself into thinking we were more clever than we were? If this wasn't some kind of elaborate trick—and I didn't think it was—maybe he'd offered us a way out.

A thin enough chance of escape perhaps but at least I didn't have to convince him we'd spoken to someone—he was convinced already. By basing his questions on a wholly incorrect assumption he'd given us breathing space we didn't deserve, and if we were to stay alive I had to make the most of it.

I thought I saw a gleam of hope in Candy's eyes but there was no discernible change in her expression.

"It was pretty bloody stupid not to think of deactivating your burglar alarm," I said, "but we're not stupid all the time." I forced more conviction into my voice. "Why the hell should I tell you what we've arranged, Inada? Candy and I didn't expect to be here long. Unless we're out of here to make a phone call you're in trouble."

Inada sipped at his drink. "I take it your disappearance will result in the disclosure of information to a third party. You have prepared written statements, perhaps?"

"Tape recordings," I lied. "We didn't have much time."

"But you know nothing about CCC."

"We know the Rochling oil depot was set on fire by an underground explosion and we know CCC was behind it. It also fits in with everything Desmond Stafford found out before you killed him."

Inada stared at me. "Tell me something I don't know, Harwood."

"What?"

"Are any of CCC's customers mentioned in your tapes?"

I had no idea what he was talking about and less idea how I should answer the question.

"We don't understand how your customer network operates," I said hesitantly.

"Ah." Inada waved a hand at Candy. "Sit down, Miss Stafford—you too, Mr. Harwood. I can see this will take some time."

Going to the desk in front of Candy he picked up one of the ledgers and opened it.

"We have spent fifteen years building up this business," he said. "Do not for a moment suppose your meddling can harm us. We have our own insurance and you will be dealt with in the same way as Miss Stafford's father. I simply asked you the question because if we are at all vulnerable it is in the area of customer relations."

"You work for the Chinese Communists, don't you?" Candy said uncertainly. "I saw their name in that book." Although she'd sat down and recovered slightly, her voice was terribly strained.

"Sometimes, Miss Stafford. Infrequently, but sometimes. You will have guessed that in Germany our fee was paid by the Red Army—or the Baader-Meinhof movement, as it is more commonly known in Europe."

By announcing his intention of killing us anyway, Inada had shaken what little confidence I had left. But I'd gone too far to stop and it would be dangerous to back off now.

"Who pays you the rest of the time?" I asked.

Inada flipped through the pages in the ledger. "Black September—you will have heard of them I'm sure, Mr. Harwood. The Palestinian Liberation Organisation—or what remains of them. Colonel Gaddafi in Libya and your old friends in the IRA, of course. More recently, the National Liberation Front in El Salvador and the South-West Africa People's Organisation." He glanced up and smiled. "Only the Africans could form an organisation having the acronym SWAPO, don't you think?" Turning back a page he studied the ledger for a moment, then spoke to Pang. "I see the Swedish people have confirmed while I have been away."

My heart was thumping. Inada had read out the names of

the most virulent terrorist groups in the world—organisations responsible for death and destruction on a huge scale.
Terrorists and guerrillas were CCC's customers—the men
keeping Inada and his company in business were the same
killers and assassins who were in the process of bringing
half of civilisation to its knees. The revelation was stagger-
ing. Now I understood Candy's horror as she'd glanced
through the ledger and at last I began to understand the
real nature of the mess we were in. Inada, Tadashi and Pang
were the masters of a company feeding on the ambitions of
bitter, violent men.

"Your customers are straightforward, bloody revolution-
aries," I said. "Call them what they are—mad bastards who
hire you to kill people."

"That is not correct, Mr. Harwood. Like you, we are
explosives experts. People die unavoidably in the course of
our business, but we are concerned principally with the
destruction of man-made structures—bridges, dams, power
stations, supertankers and air terminals—Miss Stafford has
seen the list."

"You forgot oil storage depots," I said.

"The variety is extensive," Inada replied. "Oil depots are
uncommon. So are offshore platforms and weapons instal-
lations. In some respects our customers are rather narrow-
minded."

His earlier remarks about customer relations made more
sense now. Security would be vital to CCC's sickening business. Because of the special technology that apparently allowed Inada to plant explosives wherever and whenever he
wanted, it would be easy to sell CCC's services to individu-
als or organisations who had money but no skills of their
own. But at the first hint of unreliability, China Construction would lose every contract they had.

"Did you by any chance mention our arrangement with

the Red Army in Germany?" Inada asked. "In your tape recordings?"

There wasn't a right answer to that. "Yes," I said. "At least we said we suspected as much."

Inada turned to speak to Pang. "We must take precautions and notify our German friend of possible complications. I suggest we do so immediately. If Harwood is telling the truth, the police may decide to visit us."

"There is the border device at the Lo Wu pipeline," Tadashi said. "We have protection from the Hong Kong authorities."

Inada shook his head. "The situation does not warrant such an extreme solution. I do not want to use our local investment for something which will provide no financial return."

I wondered what the hell Tadashi meant when he spoke of a device.

"What about Sweden?" Pang enquired. "Shall I request a delay?"

"Not if we can avoid it," Inada answered. "The contract is worth more than two million dollars to us. When are we required to be there?"

"Three days from now."

Inada nodded. "Then there is time to clear up matters here before planning the operation with the people in Stockholm." He turned to face me. "Mr. Harwood. Had Mr. Tadashi and I not returned to Hong Kong so quickly or perhaps if you had stayed in Germany instead of coming here, I would have taken the risk of allowing you your freedom." He blinked. "It might also have been somewhat difficult to find you."

The false tapes had failed. Inada was going to kill us anyhow. My mouth was dry and I felt sick.

"Unless he hears from us tonight Geoff Green will hand the tapes over to the West German authorities," I said desperately. "Why the hell take the risk? Let us go so I can stop him."

"Ah," Inada said. "So your colleague Mr. Green has them. The English radar expert."

"Once Green makes them public you're finished," I said. "The Germans will be on the phone in ten minutes and the Hong Kong police will take you to pieces."

"I think not, Mr. Harwood. Your story is too bizarre to sound believable. What possible reason could there be for a simple Hong Kong construction company to destroy a German oil depot?"

"Who needs a reason?" I said. "One of your employees was found shot in Candy's hotel. That links you with me and I was on contract to Rochling. Don't forget Candy and I were admitted into Hong Kong by immigration yesterday night. They'll have our names on record at the air terminal. You're being dumb, Inada. We've drawn an arrow from Rochling straight to you."

"Only if you are being truthful, Mr. Harwood. How can I be sure these tapes of yours are not entirely imaginary?"

I doubted now that he had ever believed in the tapes. Either he'd been playing with us or this was one last way to find out whether we were bluffing.

"Phone Green," I said, bluffing wildly. "Ask him if he's got the bloody things."

Inada thought for a moment. "If the tapes exist and Green has them, he will already know what they contain. A man like Green would play them whether your instructions asked him to or not."

"But as long as he hears from us he won't do anything about it," I answered. "Stop us from calling him and he'll know something's gone wrong. That's all the proof he'll need." I was losing the thread of my own argument. Everything depended on Inada's believing Geoff had tape recordings we'd never made, and unless I could convince him they

existed, Candy and I were dead. We were living a nightmare. A nightmare we'd created for ourselves and one that
was growing more convoluted and more dangerous by the
minute.

Inada spoke tersely to Tadashi. "The police must not find
them here. We may not have long. Take them downstairs
and lock them in while we arrange for the special truck."

Tadashi drained his glass, then stood up with the gun
levelled at Candy.

"Harwood," he said, "I can shoot Miss Stafford or we can
inject her with thiopental sodium. We can ship you out of
here in cardboard boxes if that's how you want it."

Slowly I moved over to the desk and helped Candy to her
feet. She was trembling uncontrollably.

"Do not believe we will misjudge you as we did in Krefeld, Harwood," Inada said. "My colleague will shoot Miss
Stafford at the slightest provocation. Is that clear?"

I nodded. "Are you going to phone Green?"

"The question is pointless. Our conversation is finished,
Mr. Harwood."

Tadashi shifted the muzzle of the automatic. "Downstairs. You first, then the girl."

Half expecting a bullet on the way out of the room, I took
Candy's hand and started walking. Would Inada phone
Geoff Green? And if he did, might Geoff guess something
strange was going on and give the right answers? How long
would it take Inada and Tadashi to make their arrange-
ments, whatever they were? How long did we have?

Maintaining my grip on Candy's hand I retreated down
the stairs until I reached the ground-floor foyer. In front of
me, on the other side of the door, the Peking Road was only
feet away. But a chasm lay between us and the safety of the
outside world. Behind, Tadashi spoke with all the confidence of a man with a gun in his hand.

"Enter the small room to your left," he said.

I went in first, waiting for Candy to join me before I turned round.

"Shut the door, Harwood." Tadashi's face was expressionless. "There is no handle on the inside."

I pushed it shut and heard the click of the lock. Candy was drenched in perspiration and couldn't stop shaking. I took her in my arms.

"They're going to kill us," she shuddered. "Just like before."

"Not yet, they're not," I said. "All the time they're worried we've got a chance. We have to think of something better than the tapes."

She stared at me. "I'm too scared to think."

I took her face in my hands. "I'm as scared as you are. No one can stop themselves being scared but you don't have to give in to it." I shook her fiercely. "Fight it."

She closed her eyes and laid her head against me. Cursing myself for ever coming to Hong Kong I tried to make myself believe there was a chance. Or would it really end like this? Instead of the bright tomorrow we'd talked of, a sudden, permanent end to everything?

I glanced around the room. No more than ten feet square, windowless and illuminated by a single bulb in the ceiling, it contrasted starkly with the opulence of the office area upstairs. With the exception of a pile of cardboard boxes and some rusty sheets of steel reinforcing mesh stacked against the far wall there was nothing I could use to mount an escape.

"How long will they be?" Candy whispered.

"Not long. They want us out of here fast."

"They didn't believe we sent tape recordings to Geoff Green, did they?"

"I don't know."

She let go of me and smoothed back her hair in an attempt to recover her composure. "Is there anything we can do?"

"What we did before. Make bloody sure we stay in one piece." I managed a smile.

"Promise me," she said suddenly. "Promise you won't do anything to make it all right just for me." She wouldn't look up.

Before I could answer, the door opened. Tadashi and Inada stood outside.

"There are cars waiting," Inada said. "One for you, Mr. Harwood, and the other for Miss Stafford. You will travel separately."

"Why?"

"Because if you are unable to assist Miss Stafford, I can be certain you will not attempt anything rash." He pointed at Tadashi's gun. "Mr. Tadashi will escort Miss Stafford. In the event of trouble he will shoot her through the wall of her stomach and in each knee-cap. I do not believe you would wish that on anyone, let alone Miss Stafford."

"Hurt her and I'll see you crucified, Inada." I spat the words at him. "Let her go, you bastard."

Tadashi came through the door and took hold of Candy's arm.

"Let her go," I yelled.

For an answer he clicked off the safety catch and thrust the muzzle of his gun hard into Candy's stomach.

She gasped and staggered backwards.

Anger and despair were threatening my ability to reason —a combination which could make me do something very dangerous. I struggled to keep calm.

"Where are you taking us?" I shouted.

"Not far." Inada nodded at Tadashi who started dragging Candy bodily out of the room.

"Candy, go with him," I said through clenched teeth. "Don't fight them. I'll see you when we get there."

Helplessly I watched Tadashi open the front door and shove her across the sidewalk to one of the cars that were double-parked outside.

"Now you, Harwood." Inada put his gun in his pocket and clamped a hand on my wrist. "Do not forget what I said about Miss Stafford. We will take the second car. The red Datsun. You will sit in the back with me."

Halfway to it I almost turned on him but Inada was ready. "Do not put Miss Stafford at risk," he murmured. "Don't do it, Harwood."

When I reached the car I wrenched the door open and climbed into the back seat not trusting myself to speak.

The lead car pulled away as Inada slid in beside me. He spoke to the driver in Chinese.

A minute later the Datsun joined the traffic stream, travelling along the Peking Road behind the car containing Tadashi and Candy.

"Inada," I said. "You might as well tell me. What are you going to do with us? I want to know."

"You and Miss Stafford are to be victims of a car accident. Mr. Pang is speaking to the Kowloon police at this very moment. He is providing the background."

"What background?"

Inada smiled coldly. "In order to safeguard the interests of our company we have no choice but to be perfectly frank with the police. Mr. Pang has gone to them to request their assistance. He is explaining what happened during his brother's recent business trip to Germany."

"What is that supposed to mean?"

"Some days ago Mr. Pang's brother accidentally overheard you speaking to Miss Stafford in a Krefeld bar. You were rather drunk and unwise enough to be bragging about a very large sum of money you had received from the Red Army terrorists. Does that set the scene for you, Mr. Harwood?"

"No."

He continued without looking at me. "Naturally, at the time, Mr. Pang's brother knew nothing of the impending disaster at the Rochling oil depot, but once the fire became front-page news, the implications of what he had overheard became clear to him. Being a foolish and somewhat reckless young man, instead of notifying the German authorities he decided to try and persuade you to hand over a portion of the money the Red Army had paid you. A dangerous and irresponsible idea, you will agree.

"When Mr. Tadashi and I learned of it, we were horrified and warned him strongly against any involvement in the matter. Are you with me now, Mr. Harwood?"

I nodded. "I think so. Shortly after you'd spoken to him Pang's brother disappeared and you and Tadashi got scared. You came back to Hong Kong so you could figure out what to do."

Inada interrupted. "Although being deeply concerned, business commitments forced us to leave without our colleague. We naturally hoped to receive a telex or cable from him saying he was all right."

"But because you haven't heard you thought you ought to contact the local police and tell them everything," I said. "Is that the story you're spinning to them?"

"Indeed it is. Mr. Pang is telling them how worried we are."

"So the police in Hong Kong will get in touch with Germany," I said, "and seeing how Pang's brother was found dead in Candy's hotel room, that more or less confirms I killed him, implicates Candy and just about proves the Red Army paid me to help them blow up Rochling."

The idea was nearly perfect. It not only removed suspicion from CCC, if in fact there had ever been any, but it placed the blame for Pang's murder and for the Rochling fire squarely on my shoulders. Better still from Inada's point of view, even if we'd made tapes, no one would ever believe them now. From our point of view the idea effectively removed the last vestiges of hope. There was only one question I wanted to ask.

"Inada, how are you going to explain why Candy and I came to Hong Kong?" I said.

"For the moment we are not aware that you are here," Inada answered. "When your bodies are discovered it will be presumed you came to silence Mr. Tadashi and me—in case we too elected to blackmail you for some of the money. Remember there were three of us together on business in Europe. You could easily have guessed we all knew of your deal with the terrorists. Having disposed of Mr. Pang to protect your credentials, it is reasonable to suppose you would wish to eliminate us as well. Your credentials as a murderer were established in Germany, Mr. Harwood. You are reputed to have been paid nine hundred thousand American dollars for your part in the fire. That is a great deal of money to someone like you."

In different circumstances I would have admired the way Inada had thought his way out of such an awkward situation. The ploy had everything, and with Pang to sell it I had no doubt it would do exactly what Inada hoped it would.

The car was crawling through the evening traffic, stopping every few yards at intersections choked with cars and people. It was dark now and Hong Kong was ablaze with neons. Directly in front of us in the other car, illuminated by the Datsun's lights, the outline of Candy's head was all that was preventing me from trying to throttle Inada. The gun was still in his pocket and the driver would have to stop the car before he could do anything to stop me. But, even if I was lucky or strong enough to choke Inada and grab his gun, unless I could force the driver to keep going Tadashi would soon know something had gone wrong.

For what seemed like hours I sat with sweat soaking

through my shirt, head pounding, while I searched for a way to keep Candy alive. Whatever Inada intended to do with us, I knew I'd never allow him to go through with it without a fight. If I was to die it would only be after I'd tried to kill Inada and Tadashi with my bare hands. The sudden flash of high explosives is a swift, clean end that in my job had never been far away. Over the years I'd learned to live with that. But a cold-blooded execution disguised as an accident was something I could not accept. When the time came, no matter what the odds, I was going to make sure it happened quickly.

Yet, as the lights of the city disappeared behind us, even this resolve began to fade and my doubts came swirling back.

Travelling due west on the main Tuen Mun highway, the traffic soon thinned and now, through the trees, there was the occasional glimpse of the ocean in the moonlight. One by one I watched signposts slip by in our headlights. Tsing Lung Tao, Anglers Beach, Dragon Beach and Brothers Point—resorts or settlements on the southern coast of the New Territories looking out towards Lan Tao.

At Pearl Island, we turned left off the highway onto a narrow side road leading down to the sea. Minutes later the driver pulled the Datsun off the road and stopped alongside the car containing Candy and Tadashi. A large refrigerated truck and a third car were parked nearby. The car had its lights on but as far as I could tell there was no one inside it. The paintwork was unusually silvery in appearance.

"You and Miss Stafford will transfer to the new car," Inada said. "You will drive."

Tadashi had already dragged Candy out of his car and was propelling her over to the one with its lights on.

Ignoring Inada I got out and ran over to her.

"What's happening?" she gasped.

"I don't know." I took hold of her arm. "Get ready to run."

Too late I saw Tadashi raise his arm. His gun smashed against my forehead before I'd begun to swing round.

Conscious but unable to stand I felt hands bundle me roughly into the car. Candy was fighting now, her screams muffled by the cotton wool which filled my head.

Astonishingly, the air inside the car was cold. So cold it took my breath away and jolted me back to life. Everything was cold. The door that slammed in my face, the seats and the steering wheel.

I heard the door shut and knew Candy was inside with me. The car began to roll.

There was a cough from the engine, then, as it took hold, we started to accelerate. The bloody thing was in gear. Grasping the wheel, I immediately tried to find the clutch pedal with my foot. But where the pedals should have been an enormous slab of ice covered the floor. It was inches thick, impossible to smash.

Wildly I hauled on the wheel only to find it was jammed solid. So were the hand brake, the gear lever, the doors and the windows. Apart from the engine, nothing worked. We were trapped in a car that had been carefully and systematically deep-frozen and we were heading for the sea.

The car was gathering speed at an alarming rate.

"Jump for it," I yelled at Candy. "Use your shoulder on the door."

As immovable as the gear lever and the steering wheel, the handle on my own door refused to budge. I made a supreme effort to free it, snapping the casting like a rotten carrot.

"The door's stuck," Candy shouted. "It won't open. Stop the car, Paul. For God's sake stop it."

There was no time left.

Travelling far too fast for the right-hand bend that lay

ahead, I braced myself for the impact. Even with steering and brakes we'd never have made it.

There was a tremendous bang. Bits of guardrail flew past the windows, then we were airborne, flying wildly out into the darkness.

TEN

The car hit the sea nose on, throwing me against the windscreen. There was a glimpse of water fountaining over the roof, a splutter from the engine, then nothing but silence and blackness.

The silence didn't last long. Water began hissing in everywhere and Candy was shouting at me again. I fought my own panic.

"Are you okay?" I yelled.

"We're sinking," she shouted. "We're sinking."

I felt my ears pop from the increasing pressure. The car was still upright but sinking faster as the water level rose inside it. Already the seats were submerged.

I tried to keep my voice steady. "Candy, are you all right?"

There was no answer and in pitch-darkness it was impossible to see if she'd been hurt.

Water was gushing through the door seals and around each window. But it was warm water. Warm Hong Kong ocean water.

Taking care not to shift my centre of gravity, I reached across and shook her. "Candy," I said. "Listen to me. Don't try and get out and don't move around. We're still the right way up and we've still got air. We mustn't upset the balance. Do you understand?"

She was rigid with fear but there was a muttered reply.

Keeping hold of her with one hand, I tried the steering wheel again. It still refused to move. Maybe it wasn't the ice that had locked the controls and sealed us in. Or if it was, maybe we'd drown before it melted and allowed us to get out.

Dizzy from the blow to my head and scared witless, I started to doubt my ability to hang on. No one could sit in a sinking car waiting to find out if the doors would open before the last bubble of air disappeared. Anyway, at the rate we were plunging towards the bottom, unless we stopped soon, even if we managed to escape, we'd never make it to the surface.

Although I couldn't see anything, as far as I could judge air pressure inside the car was beginning to balance the water pressure outside. The water was chest high now but the level wasn't rising quite so quickly.

A moment later there was a muffled, tearing noise and the car tipped slowly over onto its side.

My head was under water and I was disoriented. Candy pulled me up by my hair. "We're on the bottom," she gasped.

"Try your door again," I instructed. "The handle's over your head somewhere."

What air was left was leaking away fast.

I helped her push then quickly tried the window winder. Both were immovable.

"Pull down on the door handle," I yelled. "I'm going to kick."

I lay back with my head submerged, then rammed both feet against the door. Nothing happened.

I rose for air.

"Again," Candy shouted. "Something cracked."

The air space was so narrow I had to press my nose flat against the window to get a breath.

This time I braced myself properly and used all my remaining strength. A sudden inrush of water held me under but the ice had broken. The door was open.

I pushed Candy upwards by the ankles and followed her out.

I'd been without air too long. Fright combined with the effort of bursting the door free had used my reserves and I wasn't rising fast enough. I started counting inside my head, willing myself to reach twenty. At twenty-five the last vestiges of air bubbled from my lips. That's when I gave what I knew was a final desperate kick.

At twenty-eight, with my lungs at screaming pitch, my head broke surface and I could breathe. Frantically, I searched for Candy while I gulped oxygen. She was no more than twenty feet away from me, her head bobbing in a ring of tiny waves.

When I swam over to her she was still too breathless to speak.

"Make for those rocks," I pointed shorewards. "Quietly."

"I can't," she coughed. "Not yet. You'll have to wait a second."

From the cliff top flashlight beams licked out towards us.

"Jesus," I whispered. "They mustn't see us now. Forget the rocks. Head out to sea. Go on—you have to."

She took a breath, turned away and began swimming.

Trying to avoid any splashing I swam beside her, wondering if it was Inada and Tadashi or whether the alarm had been raised by someone else.

Twenty minutes later, with the cliff ablaze with the flashing lights of police cars and recovery vehicles, I had my answer. It was somebody else on the road to Pearl Island who had seen or heard the car smash through the guardrail and splash into the sea two hundred feet below.

By now, Inada and Tadashi would be miles away while Pang would be busy cleaning out the CCC offices in the Peking Road in case we'd been telling the truth about the tapes. Just as the ice would have melted by the time the car was recovered from the seabed, so would all traces of CCC have vanished from Kowloon.

Treading water beside Candy there was time now to think about the frozen car and realise how bloody ingenious it had been. No evidence of tampering with the doors or the controls would ever be found. No marks on the bodies to suggest the occupants had been victims of anything but an accident—a near-perfect way to dispose of the two people who had stumbled on CCC's secret. But Inada and Tadashi had miscalculated. Instead of drowning in our frozen coffin, somehow we had survived. By the grace of God, perhaps, but survive we had.

A quarter of a mile out to sea, floating amongst the seaweed and flotsam of Hong Kong's western waterway, I watched the moon climb out of Tsing Yi Island and wondered again about my luck. As it turned out I was to watch and wonder for what seemed like half the night. Once Candy had got over the shock she'd proved to be a strong swimmer and with the water at body temperature we could stay where we were until it was safe to make our move.

We came ashore to the east of Pearl Island nearly two hours after the car had taken us over the cliff. One by one the police cars and the tow trucks had abandoned the scene of the accident and not until tomorrow, in daylight, would divers try to locate the car and begin the fruitless search for bodies. We had perhaps twelve hours to decide what we were going to do. After that Inada would know that no bodies had been found.

Waterlogged and too weary to speak, we stumbled up a track of dead leaves and tree roots until we reached the main Tuen Mun highway. The second car we saw picked us up. The Chinese driver showed no surprise at our condition and took us all the way to the Miramar without asking a single question.

Candy stepped out of the shower and stood dripping water on the tiles. "Your turn," she said.

"I don't feel like getting wet again. Anyway, there isn't time. Here." I handed her a cellophane packet containing freshly laundered clothes, the same clothes we'd been wearing when we arrived in Hong Kong. They'd been delivered to our room by the Miramar's laundry service while we were out. "We'll have to wear these. At least they're dry."

"Are we going some place?" she enquired.

"Yes," I answered.

"Where?"

"I don't know. Away from here. Inada's probably taken the trouble to find out where we were staying."

"Why would he bother?" she said. "Right now he thinks we're dead."

"That won't stop him deciding to have a look through our room to see what he can find."

"In case we brought tapes with us, you mean. Do you really think he might've believed what you said about tape recordings?"

I grinned at her. "Maybe. For all we know he's been here already."

My watch was still working. It said nearly midnight. "We'll get out of the Miramar and check in to another hotel," I said. "Put on some clothes and start packing."

"I haven't got anything to pack," she said. "Anyway, I don't think we'll be allowed in anywhere else. You look terrible."

"Thanks a lot," I said. "If you'd had a gun bent round your head twice in forty-eight hours you'd look terrible, too. I have a lousy headache."

Her expression changed. "Oh Paul, I'm sorry." She took a tissue from the wall dispenser and dabbed at the split in my cheek. The salt water seemed to have done it good but where her fingers touched my face I could feel how tender it was.

She was naked and so close I could smell the freshness of her.

"Candy," I said quietly, "you're not helping." I put my arms round her and drew her to me. "I'm not sure if I know what I'm doing any more."

She looked up at me. "I don't either. It doesn't matter though. All that matters is you and me. We can't go on now. It's over. All we have to do is be with each other like you said."

I kissed her on the nose. "You're a very uncomplicated person."

She smiled. "I can handle it if you can."

Anybody who has ever defused a bomb knows how easy it is to feel lighthearted or elated after an escape of the kind we'd just experienced—easier still after three attempts on our lives in the last few days. But something was dulling the edge of it.

I kissed her again, then pushed her away. Perhaps the events of the last few hours had reversed our commitments. By suggesting everything was over, did Candy mean she really wanted to give up the search her father had begun? Had she seen the need to reach out for happiness right now —seize it with both hands, in case the future suddenly slipped away from us?

Gradually the reason for my confusion grew clearer. My involvement with CCC had gone too far. The future was already spoiled.

Tonight, I'd learned of an organisation specialising in extortion on a scale beyond the wildest dreams of any terrorist—an organisation designed to promote international tension for the sake of nothing but profit. If I couldn't forgive the methods of the IRA or the PLO, at least their leaders had a cause I could understand.

But Inada, Tadashi and Pang had no political motivation, no cause eating its way through their guts. These were men who had found a way to feed off the dreams of tyrants and dictators simply to make money. All around the world I'd tripped over dirty businesses operating outside the law. I'd met mercenaries, gunrunners, heroin dealers and hit men but I never came across anything like this. To me, at this moment, the China Construction Company seemed to be the most monstrous, the most evil, thing I'd ever encountered.

My hands still rested on Candy's waist. I wanted and needed her more than I'd ever wanted or needed anything in my life but I wasn't sure I could walk away from what I knew had to be done.

"Paul?" she queried.

"You were right all along," I said. "We've got to finish what we've started—what your father started. Not just for ourselves." I paused, unable to find the right words. "Candy, I have to stop these people. I can't just forget CCC exists—not now."

She frowned. "When you wanted us to disappear, I was ready to go with you. Now I'm so scared I want to pull out and you've decided you can't."

"Scared Inada's going to try to kill us again or scared what chasing after CCC might do to us?"

"Both." She stepped back and took a towel from the rail. "Paul, everything's changed. I'm uncomplicated enough to know when I'm out of my depth. I've proved my father was right and I've found you. Right now I don't need anything else. A year of my life's gone into this. I have twelve months to catch up on and I want to begin now—with you."

She wrapped the towel round her, then lowered her eyes. "I'd like us to make love again."

"Damn you," I said. "You're too tired, I'm too tired. You

feel that way for the wrong reason and this isn't the time or the place."

She grew more serious and slowly raised her eyes. "Then take me away."

I shook my head. "There are some lost years I have to catch up on too—remember? Maybe I can wipe out what happened in Northern Ireland and maybe I'll be able to handle the Rochling fire, but I can't start out with you while this is hanging over my head—not without trying to do something about it."

She didn't say anything.

"Candy, don't make me choose," I said.

For an answer she came to me again and put her arms round my neck. "Do you really believe I could make it without you?" she whispered.

I took a long breath. Where the hell she had come from and where the hell we were going I didn't know, but this was the best chance I was ever going to get and this time nothing was going to spoil it for me.

"Suppose you're backing a loser," I said. "There are people who'll tell you my luck gave out a couple of years ago."

"I don't think so," she answered quietly. "We'd never have escaped from the car if that was true—we wouldn't have got out of my hotel in Krefeld, either. You're no loser, Paul Harwood."

I remembered Lisa saying the same thing once—in almost exactly the same words. That was long ago, one cold winter night in England after she'd finished nursing me round from a week-long bout of drinking. I hadn't believed Lisa then and I didn't believe Candy now. There were different kinds of luck but this wasn't the time to explain.

"Okay," I said. "I'd better tell you how bad it's going to be. You put some clothes on while I get a drink. Then we'll talk it through."

"I thought we were changing hotels," she said, "in case Inada and Tadashi come here."

"After we've talked," I said, "and after I've made a phone call."

I left her and went to fix myself a drink from the fridge in the bedroom. My attempt to take on China Construction had been a disaster. Coming to Hong Kong not knowing what we were up against had nearly cost us our lives and we couldn't afford another mistake. Maybe we had ten times more information than we'd had in Germany but we were in a far worse position. This wasn't something Candy and I could handle by ourselves any longer—we needed help.

I searched for a pen and paper, then took my drink and sat down to consult the Hong Kong phone book.

By the time Candy emerged from the bathroom, I knew what we had to do.

She lay full length on the bed with her hands behind her head.

"Talk," she said.

"It's worse than you think," I said. "You can have the bad news first. While Inada and Tadashi were shoving us over the cliff, Pang was talking to the local police chief."

She raised her eyebrows but remained silent while I told her what Inada had told me during our trip to Pearl Island.

"You can bet the German and the Hong Kong police will have put the whole thing nicely together by now," I said. "I'll be on record for helping the Red Army blow up the Rochling depot—in return for my nine hundred thousand dollars. On top of that, you and I are now the confirmed killers of Pang's brother back in Krefeld. The Germans probably had us marked down for it anyway but the motive will wrap it up nicely for them. They won't know it's all lies."

"I suppose they'll know what flight we caught from Düsseldorf," Candy said. "They can find out things like that, can't they—from the emigration people?"

I nodded. "Easily. As easily as the Hong Kong police can find out we landed at Kai Tak."

"Oh." She frowned. "Then we're kind of stuck, aren't we?"

"The Hong Kong police won't be looking for us too hard," I said. "Not yet, anyway. They'll be expecting to pick us up at the air terminal on our way out. I'm more worried about Inada. Once he hears there were no bodies in the car he'll come after us again."

"Only if the police find the car," Candy said.

"They'll find it," I said. "They'll send down a couple of divers first thing in the morning."

"Okay, so we'll keep hidden. Can we do that?" She looked concerned.

"I don't know. Inada will have friends all over Hong Kong. He can probably put someone on every street corner and in every hotel lobby if he wants to. That doesn't mean he'll find us, though—Hong Kong's one big rabbit warren. Anyway, keeping one step ahead of Inada is only part of the problem—we can't just hang around and hide. Our money will run out and the longer we're here the more dangerous it's going to be."

"But we can't leave either," Candy said. "You said the police will be watching the airport."

"Rule one," I said. "If you can't run or hide—turn and fight."

She frowned again. "You mean try to kill Inada and the others before they kill us."

"No. That's not what I mean. Anyway, my guess is CCC's head office has disappeared from the Peking Road. If I'm right, we don't know where to look for them."

"So?"

"Fall back on rule two. Exploit all the information you have, no matter how thin it is."

"You're making this up as you go along," she said accusingly. "You haven't got a plan at all."

I grinned at her over the rim of my glass. "Wrong. Take a look at this." I passed her a sheet of paper.

She read aloud what I'd written on it. " 'Border device at Lo Wu pipeline. Stockholm operation in three days time. 49 211 49387.' This is a plan?"

"It is," I said. "Seeing as we have no chance of getting Inada arrested in Hong Kong whereas it's conceivable he could find us, we have to use everything we've learned about CCC's operation. That's the only card we've got to play. Remember Pang mentioned a device at the Lo Wu pipeline—some kind of a bomb, I imagine. Now I happen to know just about all of Hong Kong's water is brought into the territory from China through the Lo Wu pipeline. The authorities here might be interested to run down people who've buried a bomb near the Chinese border, don't you think?"

She nodded. "Except we can't very well go and tell anyone that. You've just said so."

"Right," I agreed. "So we either inform the police anonymously which doesn't help us at all or we use the second bit of information we've got. Inada and Tadashi said CCC are about to do a large operation somewhere in Sweden. It's going to be a hell of a lot easier to find Inada when he's working on foreign territory than it is here in Hong Kong. If it's another terrorist job, it won't be long before CCC's Swedish customers start making a noise whoever and wherever they are. That should tell us roughly where the explosives are going to be planted and you can bet CCC won't be far away from there. It depends whether my mole idea is right or not."

"But Paul, we're a million miles away in Hong Kong. The only way we're going to get to Sweden is by Chinese junk. Even if there is a way, what's to stop us being arrested by the

Swedish police the minute we arrive? The world's an awfully
tiny place when you're wanted for murder and for blowing
up a West German oil depot."

"We can't do a damn thing by ourselves," I agreed. "Not
from where we're starting. We're outgunned, outclassed
and stuck right here. Someone is going to have to help us—
someone who'll listen to us and trust us. That's what the
number is I've written down. It's an ISD phone number. We
can make the call anytime we like—direct dialling."

"To whom?" she asked quietly.

"Walter Keller, Rochling's operations manager."

She rolled over on the bed to face me. "Why not your
friend Geoff Green? What makes Keller so special?"

"He's one of the few men I respect and because Walter
Keller knows I'd never work for the Red Army. He had me
checked out while I was in Duisburg. Keller trusted me and I
trust him."

Candy shook her head. "Not good enough."

"I can ask him to take another look at the craters in
Duisburg—as long as no one's filled them in yet. Keller's
smart enough to see the explosions came from underground if I tell him what to look for."

Still her expression was one of doubt. "You'll have to
explain everything."

"I'm bargaining on him believing it."

"Paul, I've got friends in California. I can call them."
Candy sat up and swung her legs off the bed. "Keller's too
risky. You don't know him well enough."

I swallowed the rest of my scotch before I answered. "Are
your friends the kind of people who can help us out of a
mess like this? Can they get us out of Hong Kong, will they
help us find Inada in Sweden? Would they really want to get
mixed up in something they probably won't believe?"

"Why should Keller?" she asked.

"Because some bastard blew up the oil installation he was

looking after. Walter Keller won't ever be able to forget that. He'll want the truth all the way down the line, like someone else you told me about."

Her eyes widened.

"Men like Keller and your father get their jobs because of the kind of people they are," I said quietly. "I didn't know your father but I know Walter Keller."

I reached out for the phone.

Silently she passed it to me.

ELEVEN

Each day more than a hundred thousand people travel between Kowloon and Hong Kong Island by ferry. This makes Victoria Harbour one of the busiest stretches of water anywhere in the world and makes the Star Ferry terminals ideal places to lose a tail.

Here at the south end of the Kowloon public pier in the height of the morning rush hour, I was confident we'd throw off anyone who happened to have been following us. I'd explained this to Candy twice but she still had a strained look on her face.

I steered her to a vacant spot by the edge of the pier and gave her one of the sandwiches I'd bought for breakfast.

"I don't think I'm hungry," she said.

"Relax," I said. "Inada won't jump us now."

She tossed a piece of bread to a waiting seagull. "It's the crowds. I can't help it."

"We'll be there soon," I assured her. "Forget Inada."

She nodded but I knew it wasn't just Inada she was anxious about. We were on our way to an appointment at the West German consulate with no clear idea of what to expect when we got there. Last night, under the stars in Kowloon park, we'd convinced ourselves Keller wouldn't double-cross us but earlier this morning, after my call to the quiet man at the consulate, the doubts had all come back.

It was two days since I'd telephoned Walter Keller in Duisburg. Two long days to wonder if we'd done the right thing. I was sick of thinking about it and glad the waiting was over.

The seagull had ventured closer. Candy took the crust off my sandwich and scattered it in pieces along the concrete ledge beside her.

"It'll be okay," I said.

She nodded in silence.

There was more wind today, enough to kick up sizeable waves further out in the harbour. The chop hadn't reduced the number of small boats making the crossing although some of them were making heavy going of it. I watched a launch nearly swamp an overloaded junk and saw a police boat tear out of Wanchai on its way to somewhere. A line of sampans were left bobbing in its wake. It was all very scenic, very oriental and curiously unreal.

Candy pointed to a cruise ship berthed at the ocean terminal.

"How about that?" she asked.

"You wouldn't like it," I said. "People trying to escape from the real world for a while."

She smiled. "Great idea."

I handed her what remained of my sandwich. "Better leave this for your seagull," I told her. "The ferry's about to go."

We joined the stream of passengers and drifted forwards to the bow where we stood looking out at the north shore of Hong Kong Island.

A moment later, deep inside the hull, there was a rumble and water began swirling around the bow below us.

Unconscious of the spray and lost in her own thoughts, Candy stared ahead as the ferry headed out into the harbour. I stood beside her tasting the salt on my lips while my own thoughts centred on Walter Keller. Had he believed me? What had he done with the information I'd given him

and what was going to happen when we reached the consulate?

I'd been absolutely honest with Keller, starting off by
asking him to hear everything I had to say before he made
any decisions on what to do. Only once had he interrupted
—to ask if I minded if he recorded our conversation. I'd told
him to go ahead.

When I'd finished there had been no reaction—nothing
to indicate he understood or cared about what I'd told him.
At the end of the call, though, it had been Keller who'd
suggested telephoning the consulate in Hong Kong to
check for any message he might leave there for us over the
next few days. He hadn't exactly said he'd help us but he
hadn't said he wouldn't, either.

Yesterday, a girl at the consulate said she'd been expecting to hear from me, and today a quietly spoken gentleman
asked if Candy and I would agree to a meeting. Optional
rendezvous were offered, one in the open at the Man Mo
temple, another at the consulate itself.

There were two possibilities. Either the Germans had laid
a trap or Keller wanted someone in Hong Kong to check us
out face to face. Partly because we'd been given the option
of meeting elsewhere and partly because of the need to
bring things to a head quickly, I'd elected to go directly to
the consulate. Maybe the Germans were playing games with
us but in the circumstances I was prepared to take the risk.

Two hundred yards from the Hong Kong terminal the
captain swung the ferry in a long curve, put on his brakes
and engaged reverse. My admiration for the manoeuvre was
dampened by clouds of spray that swept across the deck.
Candy didn't seem to mind getting wet.

I took her hand. "We'll get off with the crowd," I said,
"just in case."

"Is it far to the consulate?" she asked.

"No. I think I know where the street is, more or less. Keep

an eye out for the Realty Building. It'll be one of these modern multistorey jobs."

Like us, most of the passengers leaving the ferry were bound for the central district. We kept pace with them, turning east onto Connaught Road until we reached the Jubilee Street intersection where I stopped to consult the map.

"We need Des Voeux Road," I said. "It's around here somewhere. Two blocks back from the waterfront."

Five minutes later we pushed our way through revolving doors to enter the air-conditioned foyer of the Realty Building. Inside it was cool and wonderfully quiet.

"Offices of the Consulate General of the Federal Republic of Germany," Candy read from a sign on the wall in front of us. "Twelfth floor."

"Okay," I said. "This is where we find out if I was right about Keller. Let's go up."

The elevator took us to the twelfth floor without stopping. Before I'd thought of anything reassuring to say, the doors opened to reveal a carpeted reception area. A pretty Chinese girl smiled at me from behind a desk. She said, "Good-morning," in English.

"My name is Harwood," I said. "Miss Stafford and I have an appointment with someone here at nine o'clock." Behind me I heard the elevator's door close.

The girl smiled again. "Yes, of course. You're expected." She stood up. "If you'd like to come with me, I'll take you through straight away."

Candy gave me a sideways glance as we followed her along a corridor to an office at the far end. The door was ajar.

"Please go in," the girl said. "I'll bring you some coffee."

The air leaking out of the office was thick with cigarette smoke.

Candy was standing apprehensively in the doorway but I

could see past her to the man waiting inside. It was Keller. I made a poor job of concealing my surprise.

He walked quickly towards me, his hand outstretched. "Ah, I suspect you were not expecting to find me here, Mr. Harwood," he said grinning broadly.

"You're Walter Keller," Candy said suddenly.

"Indeed," Keller answered. "And you are Miss Stafford. I am delighted to meet you." He shook hands with Candy. "Come and sit down, both of you. Mr. Harwood appears in need of rest. You are rather the worse for wear, my friend."

Keller was frowning at the condition of my face. I'd forgotten how it must look. The gash on my cheek was partly healed but the bruises were still a nasty colour and because we'd spent last night on a park bench I hadn't shaved.

He shut the door then helped Candy to one of the chairs grouped round a glass-topped table in the centre of the room.

"I am relieved," Keller said. "I was not sure you would come."

"We weren't, either," I admitted. "The consulate should've said you were here." I grinned at him. "Or have you come to have us arrested?"

"Not until we have several cognacs together, Mr. Harwood. And only then if you disagree with the proposals I have to make."

The remark had made Candy uneasy. Keller noticed. He lit a cigarette and leaned back in his chair. "Forgive me, Miss Stafford," he said. "My English is not good enough to attempt flippancy with someone who does not know me well. Please believe I have not travelled all this way to make things difficult for you." He smiled. "Or should I say more difficult. I am in Hong Kong because I am intrigued, because I believe we have a common cause and because I am certain we can assist each other, Mr. Harwood, I think, already understands. When you know me better I would like you to share his trust in me."

Candy flushed slightly. "We didn't know whether you'd believe us. Even Paul wasn't sure. The whole thing must have sounded crazy over the phone."

"An understatement perhaps," Keller murmured. "But what had you to gain by telling me such an extraordinary story? We live in a distorted world, Miss Stafford. The destruction of an oil depot, the death of a Chinese businessman in a Krefeld hotel—against a background of international terrorism and murder, to someone with an open mind perhaps these events are not so extraordinary as they first seem."

"Cut it out, Keller," I said. "You wouldn't be here unless you'd done some checking and at least got some answers. What have you managed to dig up?"

He stubbed out his cigarette before producing a large photograph from his briefcase. "This is a picture of Rochling's Compound Two," he said. "An aerial picture taken from a helicopter two days after the fire." He placed it on the table and slid it over to me. "You will see a number of white circles superimposed on the print. They represent the exact position of each tank before they were destroyed."

I didn't need to look. My recollection of the morning after the fire was very clear. I remembered Keller's engineer hosing debris and oil from the concrete to reveal the jagged outline of the crater. "It shows the crater is inside the perimeter of one circle," I said, "proving the charge exploded somewhere underneath the base of the tank."

"Or somewhere inside the tank," Keller remarked.

"Except you and I know it wasn't inside," I said.

He nodded. "Maybe." He laid another photograph on the table. This time I recognised the outline of the crater in the Bergedorfer Strasse. Instead of being covered with white circles, this photo was speckled with white dots. Although most of them were concentrated around the rim of the crater, fifty or sixty were scattered randomly some distance away from it.

"The dots are buried fragments of water pipe," Keller explained. "Located by means of a very powerful metal detector."

I studied the photograph more carefully.

"So dots outside the edge of the crater are bits of steel lying underneath the road surface?" I said.

"That is correct," Keller answered. "And there is only one way they could have got there as I am sure you have already realised."

I nodded. "By being driven sideways through the subsoil from an explosion originating under the road."

Keller smiled. "The road surface had perforations in it, where particles of steel were blasted upwards through it, but those particles are scattered over a wide area above ground. As I said, the white dots show the position only of fragments that are buried many metres below the ground."

It was an elegant and foolproof way to prove the explosion had originated deep below the roadway. Predictably, Keller had found a way to eliminate the doubts he must have had. These photographs would have been enough to persuade him the bombs at the depot had been in place long before I'd started my search for them.

"They are interesting pictures are they not, Mr. Harwood?" Keller kept his eyes on me while he lit another cigarette.

"Would you think so if I hadn't told you what to look for?" I asked.

"Ah," Keller laughed. "The photographs had been taken before I received your call but I had not thought to draw the position of the tanks on one and plot buried pieces of water pipe on the other. It was your remarkable theory that made me reexamine my pictures and move with some haste to see what additional evidence could be gathered. Three technicians were paid to work through the night with the metal detector to get this information. You must understand I was anxious to get here quickly."

"Paul said it was obvious the Bergedorfer Strasse crater was caused by an underground explosion," Candy said. "He could tell by looking at it."

Keller nodded. "I wished to confirm Mr. Harwood's opinion by some analytical means. Photographs are conclusive whereas I considered Mr. Harwood's opinion open to question."

"Is that why you decided to come?" Candy asked. "You believed us because of the photos?"

Keller studied the end of his cigarette. "The Rochling company is not without influence in Germany. I obtained a report on the shooting of a Chinese gentleman in the room of your hotel, Miss Stafford. You are, of course, under suspicion, especially as you are now known to have fled the country. And the police were also kind enough to supply me with a copy of a telex they had received from the FBI in Washington. It gave details of your father's occupation and explained why he resigned from his job in California. Your connection with the two fires interests the police on both sides of the Atlantic."

Candy's eyes flickered. "My father didn't resign. He was thrown out. No one believed him."

Keller smiled slightly. "Just as no one will believe me." He lifted the corner of one photograph with a fingernail. "By themselves these prove very little. The Rochling management and the German government were aware of my inability to guarantee the safety of the depot. Nevertheless, I would not expect them to accept the concept of buried explosives. Perhaps if the idea were to come from elsewhere . . . ?"

Keller didn't finish the sentence. I doubted if a man of

Keller's reputation would have been totally discredited by the Rochling fire but he was right. In his present position he couldn't offer an excuse that had so many loose ends to it.

There was a knock on the door and the receptionist entered the office carrying a tray. Keller hadn't been joking about the cognac—three coffee cups surrounded a half-full bottle of it.

He took the tray from her and placed it on the table beside the photos.

"Has the freighter radioed the message?" he asked.

"Yes, Herr Keller. Everything is in order."

He nodded. "Thank you."

When the girl had gone, Keller poured the coffee.

"You will join me?" he asked holding up the bottle.

Candy and I said we'd be pleased to. I hadn't had a drink for two days.

There was something I wanted to know. "Keller, are you here on your own account or are you here for Rochling?" I said.

Keller raised his cup in a toast. "If you mean have I explained the reason for my visit to Hong Kong to anyone, the answer is no. If you mean am I here on behalf of Rochling, then the answer is yes. In order to prevent a similar disaster from occurring in the future, I have authority to pursue whatever course of action I consider necessary to report on the fire." He paused for a moment. "On this particular matter I also have a degree of official backing from the Federal government."

"Even though you haven't told them about us?" Candy gave him one of her direct stares.

Keller smiled slightly. "Millions of dollars of damage to the Rochling depot is one thing, the Baader-Meinhof movement is another. I have mentioned only that I have confidential information which I wish to pursue. A lead, I think you would call it, Miss Stafford. The Bonn government is usually prepared to support any attempt to obtain hard information about the activities of our Red Army terrorists."

"The China Construction Company doesn't have much of a connection with the Red Army," I said.

"Sufficient, Mr. Harwood. Sufficient." Keller poured himself more cognac. "Tell me more about this Hong Kong company. I am particularly interested in the concept of a hydraulic burrowing machine you mentioned on the telephone."

I'd worked with Keller long enough to know when he was flying a kite.

"You don't buy the idea, do you?" I said.

"I am fascinated," Keller answered. "But I had neither the time nor the resources to check for evidence."

"It's only an idea," I said.

He nodded. "Together we shall improve upon it, perhaps. Let us review the whole affair from the beginning. I imagine we should start with Miss Stafford. She has been involved with all this much longer than you or I have." He turned to Candy. "I believe Mr. Harwood and I have a great deal to thank you for."

Candy smiled at him. "You might have trouble getting Paul to agree with that."

Talking slowly, she began by telling Keller about the fire on Rough and Ready Island, going on to describe her father's death and explaining how she'd decided to find someone to help her prove his theories. I took over the narrative from the point where Candy had arrived at the door of my hotel room that cold, grey Duisburg morning after the fire.

By the time we'd finished, we'd emptied the cognac bottle and Keller's ashtray was close to overflowing. He'd listened intently, occasionally closing his eyes when he wanted to concentrate or sort out something that bothered him.

Just having Keller here had made all the difference. As

well as giving the impression of wanting to help, he'd obviously come to Hong Kong with some firm ideas on what to do next.

I stood up to stretch. "Okay," I said. "What now?"

"I listed my thoughts while on the plane," Keller said. "From what you have told me this morning, I see no reason to modify them. Would you care to hear what they are?"

"We were kind of relying on you," Candy said quietly. "Paul and I can't do anything more by ourselves. We can't even get out of Hong Kong."

Keller took a sheet of paper from his case. "Leaving Hong Kong will not be difficult. I have brought fresh passports for you. The embassy will attend to photographs and other matters."

In my wildest optimism I'd never expected this kind of support. Candy was equally astonished. She began to say something but changed her mind.

Keller was unmoved by our reaction. "There is a more serious problem," he continued. "Even though you will be able to provide descriptions of them, Inada, Tadashi and Pang will not be easy to run down. If they suspect you did not drown, they may decide it unwise to travel to Stockholm. Also I believe you mentioned telling them about some tape recordings left with Mr. Green in Duisburg. That will concern them greatly."

I'd neglected to explain that there weren't any tapes.

"I think CCC will go ahead, anyway," Candy said suddenly. "Inada said the job in Stockholm was worth two million dollars to them. He knows there can't be anything on the tapes about Sweden. We only heard about it after we'd got here."

Candy's remark implied that we really had left tapes with Geoff Green.

Keller interrupted before I could correct the impression. "Inada may have assumed you would telephone Green with the information," he said. "Perhaps he has even guessed you called me."

I shook my head. "I don't think so. We thought it was risky phoning anyone. Inada would never expect me to try and contact anyone at Rochling after what's happened."

"But what about Mr. Green?" Keller repeated. "Your English colleague—or one of Miss Stafford's friends?"

"Even if we had, it's not likely we could make trouble for CCC in Sweden," I said. "Not while we're wanted for murder and God knows what in Germany."

Keller nodded. "True. Nevertheless, it will be safer and better if everyone believes you both to be dead—drowned in the car at Pearl Island. Do you not think so?"

"Sure," I said. "But there's not a hell of a lot we can do about it now."

Keller rose stiffly to his feet and inspected an empty cigarette packet. "There is a slim hope," he said. "The principal reason I travelled here so rapidly." He paused.

I resisted the temptation to prompt him.

"It is late but not too late for bodies to be found, Mr. Harwood. Washed up some distance from Pearl Island perhaps. Had you thought of that?"

I grinned at him. "No. I'm impressed with the passports but I really don't think the German consulate can produce dead bodies to order."

Keller answered. "Indeed. That is rather what they said. Instead they recommended an alternative."

"What sort of alternative?" Candy asked.

"Shortly after your arrival here this morning, a departing German freighter radioed a report concerning the recovery of two bodies floating off Mong Han Shek. A man and a woman, both European. Credit cards in the man's wallet bear the name Paul Harwood but the captain regrets he is unable to identify the woman positively." Keller smiled at Candy. "The body of the young lady is in somewhat less than perfect condition but I understand it bears a remarkable likeness to you, Miss Stafford. The consulate general is confident the authorities will not bother to recall the vessel. She already nears the limit of Hong Kong's territorial waters."

"Christ, Keller," I said. "Where were you before you worked for Rochling—military intelligence?"

He raised his eyebrows but said nothing.

"Why exactly are you doing all this, Mr. Keller?" Candy asked quietly.

He looked surprised. "Surely the reasons are obvious. To make certain CCC proceed with their next project and to make certain there are no barriers to prevent you and Mr. Harwood from accompanying me to Stockholm. I must learn the truth about the fire at Rochling, you and Mr. Harwood must clear yourselves from the accusations which are currently levelled against you and, above all, the organisation you call CCC must be brought to justice."

Two days ago, when I'd phoned Keller from the Miramar, I deliberately hadn't mentioned my idea of hunting down CCC in Sweden. I hadn't mentioned it this morning, either.

Already my confidence in this dour German had been repaid and already the fresh beginning I'd promised Candy was in my sights.

"Keller," I said. "We need more cognac."

TWELVE

The wind was coming off the North Sea, driving inland under a leaden sky to chill everything in its path. Stockholm had been cold enough but out here on the west coast the wind was biting through my parka like a knife. Hong Kong was a million miles away and it seemed a lifetime ago I'd taken the job at Rochling to pay for a winter somewhere in the sun.

Candy's fur-lined hood was flecked with snow and even Keller was stamping his feet and shivering. The three of us were slowly freezing to death and we were wasting our time. Unless we had some idea of where to look and what to look for, all the metal detectors in Sweden weren't going to help.

I waited for one of the big Volvo trucks to rumble by before I spoke to Keller again. His face was pinched in the cold.

"I think our friends will soon give up," he said. "They are beginning to share our pessimism."

"If it hasn't got a steel shell, the best detector in the world won't pick it up," I said. "Anyway, for all we know it's fifty feet down."

He cupped his hands and tried unsuccessfully to light a cigarette. "In English you call it a fool's errand, do you not?" he said. "A search for something that either does not exist or that is impossible to find if it does."

Fourteen vehicles were being used in a systematic search for the explosives. Fourteen vehicles, fifty men and two sniffer dogs to locate a package of dynamite which at any moment could cause an explosion that would make the Rochling disaster look like a firework.

Far below us, deep in the sedimentary rock of Gothenburg's Hjartholmen island, lay the world's largest artificial cave—four interconnected caverns, each sixty feet wide, a hundred feet high and fifteen hundred feet long. A huge thirty-six-million-cubic-foot hole that had cost the Swedish taxpayers four billion dollars.

At first when Keller had described the caverns to me, I'd thought he'd been exaggerating. My work in Duisburg had taught me something about storing oil in tanks above the ground but no one had told me there were other ways of doing it. Even after I'd seen the photographs and drawings in Stockholm, I hadn't appreciated the true size of the Hjartholmen oil storage complex.

Here, not far from the city of Gothenburg, hundreds of millions of gallons of fuel oil floated on water beds so far underground they were invulnerable to attack from the most powerful nuclear warhead. Not even a direct hit could penetrate the hundreds of feet of solid rock guarding Sweden's precious oil reserves. Yet in the last few days some Swedes had begun to doubt the safety of their storage system. Yesterday, after speaking to the manager of a German oil depot that had been recently destroyed by an underground bomb, doubt had given way to nervousness and by today nervousness had turned into something close to panic.

Keller had managed to light his cigarette. He squinted out over the eerie landscape of excavated rock searching for an answer I knew he wouldn't find.

"Come on," I said. "It's too damned cold out here. We're not doing anything useful standing around like this. Let's go inside. Tegholm's waiting for us."

He nodded. "If we are going to talk, please do not forget

you are a German mining engineer and that Miss Stafford is supposed to be a geologist."

His reminder was unnecessary. We'd travelled to Stockholm on new passports supplied by the German consulate and we'd had plenty of practice on the journey. Both Candy and I had dyed our hair and Candy's had been cut short. She didn't look much like a German geologist but she didn't look like Candy Stafford, either.

Whether or not our identities would stand up to close examination was open to question, but the staff of the refinery were preoccupied with the emergency and they had no reason to suspect we weren't who Keller said we were.

"If you're going in, I'd better get someone to drive me into Gothenburg," Candy said. "I promised to help make up those identikit pictures."

"Okay," I agreed. "Keller and I are going to talk to Tegholm again. I'll phone you after the boat trip."

We began the walk back to the only part of the Hjartholmen complex visible above the ground—a squat concrete building housing the pumps and control instrumentation for the whole complex. Once off the roadways, walking around Hjartholmen wasn't easy. Boulders and crushed rock littered this part of the island, the residual debris from the millions of cubic feet of rock that had been excavated to make the caverns.

Sven Tegholm met us at the entrance. He was the manager of the underground store—a tall, thin man who had begun to show signs of cracking under the strain.

"Nothing?"

Keller shook his head. "I think it will be more useful to direct our effort elsewhere. Perhaps you have new information from Stockholm?"

"Not yet," Tegholm answered. "But let us not talk out here in the wind. I can see you are all very cold."

"I have to go in to your head office in Gothenburg," Candy said. "You need the pictures."

"Ah, yes. If you will wait just a moment I will arrange for a driver. Are you sure you will not have a hot drink before you leave?"

"No, thank you," Candy smiled. "I'll go right away if that's alright."

"Of course, Fräulein Klemm, but of course." He spoke into a radio transmitter clipped to his lapel.

Klemm was Candy's new name. For a brief few days in Hong Kong she'd been Anne Gregory—now she was Ingrid Klemm, a geologist from Frankfurt with a passport to prove it. My new name was Studer, Hans Studer. I didn't like mine any better than I liked Candy's but for the time being they were a good deal safer than Paul Harwood and Candy Stafford.

"I'll go straight back to the hotel afterwards," Candy said. "I'll stay there until you call me."

The driver was waiting for her.

I resisted the temptation to accompany her to the car. Outwardly our relationship was that of colleagues on business in a foreign country and I didn't want to give Tegholm any ideas. We'd adopted the pretence intuitively, either because it seemed a sure way to avoid mistakes in front of our Swedish hosts or perhaps because the artificiality of our new names was a constant reminder to be careful.

I waved good-bye to Candy, then followed Keller and Tegholm into the building. It was comfortably stuffy inside, and after the howling of the wind there was something friendly in the subdued hum from the battery of pumps connecting the caverns to the refinery and Torshamnen harbour.

Tegholm began to say something in Swedish but corrected himself. "Come, gentlemen, we shall discuss our internal examination of the store." He led us to a small office that smelt of fuel oil and stale coffee.

English was a common language for Keller and Tegholm and, apart from the odd stumble, both men spoke it easily without having to think. My English and Candy's American had impressed Tegholm but so far not to the point where we'd been forced to use prearranged cover stories to explain our fluency.

I stripped off my parka, then joined Keller who was studying a large photograph on one of the walls.

"It gives visitors an impression of the store," Tegholm said. "Many people are disappointed to learn they are not permitted below ground, so we have taken many pictures to show them."

"Tegholm, how long do we have?" Keller asked. "You must have some idea."

The Swede spread his hands. "I do not know. Your guess will be better than mine. We are not accustomed to circumstances of this kind in Sweden. Your experience in Germany places you at an advantage." He was suddenly embarrassed. "Please understand, my colleagues and I deeply regret what occurred at Rochling. I mean only to say we are fortunate to have you here, Herr Keller. Without the information you have given us how could we have known what to do?"

The emergency, as Tegholm called it, had been well under way before our plane had touched down in Stockholm last night. In fact, although we hadn't been aware of it then, the situation was already so critical that by calling the Ministry of Foreign Affairs to give warning of a possible terrorist threat, Keller had caused a bloody uproar. Minutes after he'd put the phone down police had arrived to collect him from our hotel, leaving Candy and me to bite our nails until he'd returned exhausted at one o'clock in the morning.

Despite this unnerving beginning to our visit, once Keller had established his credentials and explained why we were here, the Swedish authorities had grasped him like drowning men. In the haste to transfer us all to Gothenburg the following morning, questions about the two German specialists Keller had brought with him had been less than searching, and if Swedish efficiency didn't quite match that of the Germans, it was still impressive. Whether it was impressive enough to protect Hjartholmen from one of CCC's invisible bombs depended largely on the reaction to advice Keller had given Tegholm.

The advice was simple. Instead of searching for explosives, find Inada before he triggered the detonator. And if Tegholm had listened, protecting Hjartholmen would have been a hell of a lot easier than trying to protect the Rochling depot.

As it turned out, Tegholm seemed determined to search for explosives that were almost certainly unfindable and he'd been reluctant to bother with identikit sketches of Inada and Tadashi that could already have been distributed to the refinery's security team if the Swedish manager had been faster on his feet.

The hunt for evidence of a buried bomb had been singularly unsuccessful. Keller said he'd been forceful to the point of being rude when he'd told Tegholm a conventional search would be pointless, but the Swedish manager had insisted on using metal detectors in an attempt to locate a package of plastic explosives that probably had no more than a few ounces of metal in it. The next step was more enterprising but equally unlikely to yield results. It had the added disadvantage of needing my participation.

The search for people had been more rewarding. Although none of the hotels in Gothenburg had Chinese guests and we'd drawn a blank with the car-hire companies, of one thing we were sure: Inada and Tadashi were here somewhere. They'd entered Sweden four days ago on their own passports and they weren't here on holiday.

Tegholm placed a finger on the photo. "Herr Studer," he said. "These are the pipes I told you about. All three are visible in this picture. This one in the centre descends to a sump in the bottom of the main cavern. We use it to remove ground water which seeps into the store through fissures in the rock. Alternatively, we can reverse the flow and pump water back into the caverns through it."

"That's how you control the oil level, isn't it?" I said.

Tegholm nodded. "The oil is floating on a layer of water. To prevent an inflammable mixture of vapour and air from forming above the surface of the oil, the correct quantity of water is added to keep the caverns full to the roof at all times."

For the everyday operation of an underground system it was a neat way of avoiding the explosion hazard but Tegholm had overlooked something. We weren't here to solve an everyday problem and Tegholm hadn't seen the bent and twisted tank tops littering the Rochling compound the morning after the Duisburg fire.

"And the other two pipes?" I asked. "They're for oil in and oil out, are they?"

"One comes from Torshamnen. Fuel oil is discharged into it directly. The pipework and the pumps have the capacity to empty a two-hundred-thousand-tonne ocean tanker in less than twenty-four hours. The outlet pipe carries oil from the cavern to the refinery for cracking. As you can see, it is all very simple."

"How much water have you pumped out of the store?" Keller asked.

Tegholm smiled. "All that we can. Fortunately we do not have a full complement of oil at the moment. We are awaiting the arrival of three tankers from the North Sea. There will be about twelve metres between the surface of the oil and the roof of the caverns. It increases the danger but we will be careful." He paused. "Shall we get ready, Herr

Studer? I wish to pump water back into the store as soon as possible."

A tiny knot had formed in my stomach while Tegholm had been talking. I'd been underground before but not in an oil-filled cave. "There's something we ought to clear up first," I said. "I don't think it makes any difference if the store is full or not. If we're dealing with a buried charge of explosives, we're in trouble either way."

Tegholm didn't understand. Keller pretended not to but he knew damned well what I was going to say.

"Please explain," Tegholm said.

"Okay. Imagine the store's partly empty as it is right now, with millions of cubic feet of potentially explosive vapour filling the space over the top of the oil. You don't need dynamite to ignite that—if there's the right amount of air mixed with the vapour, a single spark will do it. You'll be able to say good-bye to the whole island."

"Which is precisely why I am anxious to refill the store with water, Herr Studer," Tegholm said patiently. "We are aware of the hazard. I do not see what you are getting at."

"Pumping water back in won't help," I said. "Not if the charge is where we think it is. Sure you'll get rid of the vapour-air mixture and you'll have your caverns crammed with oil floating nicely on its water bed. Great, except that oil and water are incompressible. What happens now if there's a bloody great explosion somewhere in the roof or the walls of the cavern? What about the pressure wave?"

Keller raised his eyebrows. Tegholm's expression had slipped. He bit nervously on his lip.

"The roof of the cavern will crack open," he said eventually. "Thousand of tonnes of rock will fall into the oil."

"And the oil will catch fire," Keller remarked. "There will be waves, foam and aerosol mist."

"Then we shall carry out our inspection at once," Tegholm said. "We should not waste any more time. I fear

you are right about the consequences of an explosion, Herr
Studer. Let us pray we can stop such a terrible thing from
happening. Please wait here while I see if the suits are
ready."

When he'd gone Keller lit a cigarette.

"You were supposed to leave your lighter and matches at
the gate," I reminded him.

"Your Chinese friends are not relying on cigarettes and
matches, Mr. Harwood. I shall smoke while you and
Tegholm carry out your inspection. I hope you enjoy yourself."

"If the island disintegrates while I'm in there, I'll blame
you," I said. "I notice you didn't volunteer."

"I am too old," Keller grinned. "And I do not believe
there is anything to see. The key to this assignment is Inada.
Find him and we will have solved Tegholm's problem."

"Look, Keller," I said. "You must have some idea how
long we've got. What did the people in Stockholm have to
say about it?"

"They said it is possible the whole thing is a bluff. It was
not until Swedish immigration confirmed entry of Inada
and Tadashi that anyone was sure. I myself prefer to believe
we have more time than Tegholm thinks. The people who
are threatening to destroy the Hjartholmen oil store are not
terrorists, they are businessmen. They will not act in haste,
and only then if they have no option."

"Don't you think the government will try and buy time?"

"No," Keller answered, "not unless they can keep the
matter secret. They are in serious trouble with their nuclear
power programme as it is. The environmentalists and Swedish people will never allow their uranium to be mined, especially for export."

Neither Keller or Tegholm had said much about the poli-
tics behind the threat to destroy Sweden's largest underground oil store. I knew only that Sweden was sitting on ten

percent of the world's uranium reserves and that for some time the government had been under pressure to boost a flagging economy by mining the deposits. Until recently the pressure had come from inside Sweden, but in the last month things had taken a much more sinister turn.

At the briefing yesterday Keller had been shown a series of letters the government had received from a consortium of unnamed businessmen. Apparently, the first letter had suggested the destruction of Sweden's indestructible oil storage system would reinforce the case for building more nuclear reactors. Fuel for the reactors could be readily extracted from Sweden's own deposits of uranium, the letter argued, and once mining had started, the consortium would be pleased to introduce overseas customers to the Swedish government. Since then, more letters had been delivered, each more explicit than the one before. The whole thing sounded like extortion on a grand scale—an ideal set-up for CCC.

"In some ways I have little sympathy for the Swedes," Keller observed. "They chose not to become a member of NATO, and third-world nations who are desperate for uranium to construct nuclear weapons or fuel their reactors will always believe it easier to blackmail a non-aligned country."

Tegholm had returned and had overheard the remark without Keller knowing. He was visibly annoyed. "Herr Keller, Sweden is an armed neutrality with special responsibilities. Our position is quite different to that of Europe. I suggest you ask our Finnish neighbours what they think of Swedish policy."

"I had not intended to criticise," Keller said quietly. "Half my own country is controlled by the East. I understand the delicacy of the Finnish situation very well. Herr Studer and I were merely discussing how long we have to act. I was endeavouring to explain my own thoughts on the matter."

"It is unimportant," Tegholm said. "Stockholm has telexed a warning. They believe a demonstration of strength is imminent—perhaps something that falls short of an attempt to destroy the store."

"Great," I said. "If Inada and Tadashi are going to practice, maybe we can get them on their demonstration run. Do all your men know what to look for?"

Tegholm nodded. "There are fifty men on the island and another sixty-eight of the special service on watch elsewhere. The refinery and the harbour are also being guarded." He frowned. "I believe you mentioned the possibility of remote detonation, Herr Studer, did you not—by means of a radio signal?"

"That's right. I think CCC might fire their charges by using a radio transmitter."

"Over what range?" Tegholm asked.

"I don't know. We're almost sure CCC was operating from a van parked outside the main gate at the Rochling depot. That's not too far."

A man poked his head round the door and spoke to Tegholm in Swedish.

"Everything is ready," Tegholm announced. "If you will put out your cigarette, Herr Keller, you can accompany us to the manhole."

"I'll stay here," Keller said. "Let me know if you find anything."

I told him he was a cynical bastard, then accompanied Tegholm to what he called the changing room.

It was a small room containing a winch driven by compressed air and a wooden table on which our equipment was laid out. In the centre of the floor was the single means of entry to the caverns—a circular manhole covered by a steel lid. Two of Tegholm's men were busy greasing the winch.

The manhole lid was shut but the stench of oil was powerful enough to make me choke. My eyes were stinging and the fumes weren't helping the squirming in my stomach.

It took twenty minutes to prepare ourselves. The woollen underwear was bearable when I first put it on but the tight-fitting dry suit quickly increased the pressure on my skin until every fibre was scratching me at the same time. Tegholm didn't seem to notice the discomfort. He helped me adjust my face mask, then stood aside while his men checked me over.

Hydrocarbon vapour is nasty stuff. Even low concentrations are toxic and you don't need to inhale much to wind up dead. If there was a pressure drop in my air supply system, enough vapour to cause narcosis of my nervous system could leak in through the tiniest hole in my mask. Soon after that I'd suffer lung damage and fall into a coma. Tegholm and Keller had both told me the coma would be fatal. I hoped Tegholm's men could see what they were doing. They were coughing badly from the fumes and had tears running down their faces.

I lifted back the lid on the manhole and shone my light through the hole to see how far we'd have to be lowered. The rubber dinghy was already down there, floating on a smooth, black mirror forty feet below. Because I was breathing clean air from the tanks on my back, I couldn't smell the vapour pouring out of the hole but even through the suit I could feel how bloody cold it was.

Tegholm went first. He carried a big floodlight in one hand and had a pair of oars lashed across his tanks. I watched him swing sideways on the rope until he caught the dinghy with his foot to steady himself. When he waved his light the men lowered him the last few feet. Ripples spread outwards from the dinghy, travelling slowly over the lake until they disappeared into empty blackness.

It was my turn now. I'd done some unusual things in the

last few years but rowing around an underground sea of fuel oil in a rubber dinghy wasn't one of them. The novelty value was high but overshadowed somewhat by the thought of Inada crouched in a van somewhere with his finger resting on a button.

Taking care not to dislodge my mask, I eased myself through the hole on my stomach until I was hanging by the rope. I nodded at the winch driver. There was a hiss from the air motor followed by a sudden jerk. Then I was on my way down.

The rope was biting into my armpits through the suit. In trying to ease the pressure I succeeded only in dropping my light. But I was nearly there. Tegholm caught the flashlight and guided my feet into the dinghy. I gave him the thumbs-up to say thank you.

It wasn't until I'd untied the rope and sat down that the immense size of the main cavern became apparent.

We were at one end of it, equidistant from the side walls and not too far from the cluster of huge service pipes I could just see with my light. Everything was red, a translucent, dull red. The walls were red, the curving arch of the cavern roof was red and when I shone my flashlight downwards the lake sucked the beam into it in a glowing ball of opalescent red.

The dinghy was slippery with oil. Drips from the roof had already smothered my suit and smeared my mask so badly it was difficult to see at all. Wiping the glass made little or no difference.

There was no novelty value. This was not a place for men. Devoid of breathable air, bitterly cold and dripping in oil, the bowels of Hjartholmen were surely unlike anywhere else on earth. Here on the west coast of Sweden, mining engineers had constructed these frozen halls to contain oil and I felt strongly that no one should be doing what Tegholm and

I were doing. Clenching my teeth to stop them chattering I tried to remember why we were here.

Tegholm had stopped rowing and was using the big light to inspect the cavern roof. Enormous blocks of rock hung above our heads, some of them dangerously fissured from the blasting operations. Even through the film of red oil that smothered everything, the texture of the roof appeared frighteningly coarse. Not a square inch of it was smooth. Explosives had shattered the rock to pieces and there had been no need for anyone to improve on the finish the dynamite had left behind.

Tegholm handed me a plastic squeeze bottle, indicating I should use it to clean my mask. I did as he instructed and found I could see again. Whatever the bottle contained, it not only removed the film from the glass but it washed the oil from my gloves so I wasn't so frightened of dropping the flashlight.

Like a steep sculpture in some dreadful subterranean world, the three gleaming pipes rose out of the oil. I tried to think of them as a connection with the surface. But they were as alien as the lake itself and they were as much a part of this foreign environment as the oil was.

By directing my light along the cavern I persuaded Tegholm to start rowing again.

We were no more than two hundred feet from the cluster of pipes when the unthinkable happened.

Far above us there was a brilliant flash of light accompanied by a long and terrifying roar. And, as if in slow motion, thirty feet of rock peeled off the cavern roof.

Through a hail of debris and dust I saw it swallowed up in a giant fountain of oil. Then I watched the tidal wave climb the sides and come towards us like a wall.

There was time to clamp my mask against my face, then

the wave picked up the dinghy like a toy and I was fighting for my life.

Seized by uncompromising terror, I kicked out wildly, trying to stay on the surface. But this wasn't water and the oil wouldn't support me. Enveloped in silky smooth blackness I was sinking to my death at the bottom of the cavern.

For a second I fancied my arm splashed through the surface. But there was no surface. In such utter darkness with my mask smothered in oil, the surface was unidentifiable.

Again panic took hold of me and for a second time I thrashed around until the rasping of my breath brought me to my senses. I was disoriented now—unable to determine which way was up.

Was I ten feet down? Twenty? If I ripped off the tanks would I gain enough buoyancy to rise to the surface? And if I ever reached it without them, how many gulps of vapour would it take to kill me?

Slowly I experimented with my arms and legs, moving them in what I believed might be a way to swim through fuel oil. After a couple of minutes I imagined I was making headway. The pressure of my ears reduced and for a moment the panic eased. But would my air last out? Where was the manhole?

The blackness was awful and I had no idea which way to go. Fear was returning when my gloves tangled in steel netting. Frantically I pulled myself towards it, clinging to the mesh with all my remaining strength.

At once I felt the net begin to move.

My feet slid from the oil and I knew I was on the journey upwards to the manhole.

In the changing room, hands clamped my arms to my side, then suddenly I could see again.

Tegholm's men were using a high-pressure jet of petrol to hose me down. Beside the manhole the rescue net lay in an oily heap and there, standing beside it, still in his suit, was Tegholm. He raised a hand as if in greeting.

Fumes had leaked in through my mask—or perhaps my air tanks were exhausted.

The shutters came down before I could return his wave.

THIRTEEN

I woke up not knowing where I was. Even after I'd heard Candy answer the phone I wasn't sure. The effects of the sedative hadn't worn off and it took several seconds to get my head working.

I swung my feet out of bed, stood up and made my way unsteadily into the lounge.

She was standing by the window with the receiver hanging loosely in her hand. Sunlight was pouring into the room, hurting my eyes.

"Is that Keller?" I asked.

"Yes."

"Let me speak to him."

Her expression didn't alter. "I've told him you're not going back to the island."

"Candy," I said. "We're within an ace of cracking it. I have to talk to him."

"I'm not letting you go back there. Tegholm can do it. There's something I have to tell you."

Gently I took the receiver from her. She didn't try to stop me.

"What is it, Keller?" I said.

His German accent was more pronounced and he sounded very tired. I listened to what he had to say, then hung up.

Candy looked at me.

"It was in the plug," I said. "Tegholm took a team back in last night. They've got photos."

Now it was confirmed, it was hard to believe I could ever have been so stupid. There wasn't any magic—there never had been. No remote-controlled mole and no warhead deposited at the end of an underground tunnel. CCC's operations relied on nothing more sophisticated than patience and good planning. I sat down wondering why the hell I hadn't thought of it right at the beginning. The evidence had been staring me in the face at the Rochling depot but somehow I'd managed to miss it completely.

"Are you going back to Hjartholmen?" Candy asked softly.

"No. Keller's handling it, he's out there now."

"You didn't hear me, did you? I said I had something to tell you." She sat down beside me. "Hold out your arm."

"What for?"

Her eyes flashed. "You know what for."

I did as she said, trying to stop the telltale wavering at my fingertips.

"Paul, we've done enough. You nearly died in there. So did Tegholm. Someone else can finish it for us. We can't stay here."

Candy wasn't making sense, Keller didn't know what to do out on the island and I couldn't concentrate on anything without my head pounding. Worse still, I didn't want to think—not about staying here, not about Hjartholmen and above all not about yesterday. The nightmare was as fresh this morning as it had been when they'd brought me back half dead to the hotel yesterday afternoon. Last night I hadn't been able to close my eyes or turn off the light without shaking, and if I let it, the feeling returned immediately—the sucking smoothness of the oil, the dreadful cloying blackness and the roar of breath inside my mask as I fought to keep on the surface.

Candy's next question brought me back out of the cavern. "What else did Keller say?"

"He's going to try and X-ray the plug. Tegholm thinks there's another bomb in it."

She was picking at a loose strand of cotton on her blouse.

"What is it you're trying so hard not to say?" I made her look at me.

"Geoff Green's dead."

I dug my fingers into the sofa until they hurt. "How do you know?"

"Yesterday when I came back here—I phoned the electronics company you said he worked for in England. I was going to ask if he'd fly to Gothenburg." She stopped abruptly.

"Because you thought something had gone wrong—is that why?"

She nodded. "I wasn't sure before but I am now."

"Go on."

"He never got out of Germany. The man I spoke to said his body was found in a car near the Rhine. He'd been shot through the head."

"Jesus Christ," I said through clenched teeth. "He was murdered in case he knew what he knew. Inada and Tadashi killed him. The bastards killed him." I was choking on my anger.

"Paul. It wasn't Inada. I asked when it had happened. Inada and Tadashi weren't in Germany when Geoff Green was shot. They'd left two days before. They were in Hong Kong."

Rage sharpened my ability to think. "Inada must've thought we were telling the truth about the tapes after all," I said bitterly. "Or thought we might have been."

"And decided to play safe," Candy finished the sentence for me. "They arranged for someone in Germany to kill Geoff Green for them."

I willed her to say more but I knew she wasn't going to.

"I couldn't tell you when they brought you back from the island," she said. "I had to wait until this morning."

"What made you decide to ask Geoff to come here to start with?" I said. "You hadn't even met him."

She looked embarrassed. "It's hard to explain. I just had the feeling things were getting out of control somehow. We're not doing anything by ourselves any more. Keller's doing all the organising."

"That was supposed to be what we wanted," I said. "He's keeping us in the background deliberately. Keller's making sure no one starts wondering who we really are. Don't forget Inada and Tadashi are in Gothenburg, too."

Candy was frowning. "It's not just that. Everything's happened too fast. Three days ago we were in Hong Kong and now we're in Sweden. Keller's taken over."

"We asked him to," I said. "We didn't have any choice— remember? You still haven't said why you phoned Geoff."

"Because I know you trusted him and because he could have figured out how to locate a radio transmitter if that's what Inada's using. If Geoff had been here, we'd have had a chance to trace the signal yesterday, wouldn't we?"

Candy was hedging. I could accept her feelings of uneasiness but there was more to it than that.

"Have you got some idea who killed Geoff?" I said.

She reddened slightly. "No."

"For Christ's sake," I said angrily, "if you've got something to say—say it. We're trying to stop a bloody island from blowing up."

"You won't believe me."

"Believe what?"

Her mouth was set in a firm line.

"Candy," I said. "Just tell me."

"I think Walter Keller killed Geoff Green."

I stared at her incredulously. "You're crazy."

"I said you wouldn't believe me." She looked angry.

"What the hell do you expect?"

"I don't know."

"Do you have any proof?"

"No. I can build an argument that convinces me, but I know you won't believe it." She refused to meet my eyes.

I managed to stop myself from answering. Her indictment of my ability to accept her suspicions came as something of a shock and although I couldn't believe she was right about Keller, Candy would never have tried to phone Geoff unless she was deeply worried.

"I'm not usually one-eyed," I said.

"About Keller you are." She swung round. "I don't know anything for sure, but I'm scared, Paul."

I stared at her. "I didn't want to listen once before, did I? A couple of hundred years ago in Duisburg. You'd better tell me—even though the whole thing's crazy."

She shook her head. "No, it's not. The men who made up the identikit pictures didn't know what they were doing it for. I don't think Keller's told Tegholm the truth. We haven't any idea what Keller said to Tegholm in Stockholm because we weren't involved in the meetings, were we?"

"Then why did Keller come to Hong Kong when we phoned him?"

Even before she started to reply, I knew what Candy's answer was going to be. If Keller, for some impossible reason, had been working with CCC all along, he'd rushed to Hong Kong to make sure we didn't tell anyone else what we knew. Could our phone call to Germany really have blown everything?

"Keller was on our side," she went on, "that's what we thought, wasn't it? So we've gone along with anything he's wanted. He's kept us quiet without us realising it."

"He didn't have to get us new passports and bring us to Sweden," I reminded her. "If Keller told Inada he knew where we were, CCC could've had another go at killing us in Hong Kong."

She shook her head again. "Not after we'd visited Keller officially at the consulate—that would've been too dangerous. Anyway, I'm sure he's trying to find out if we really made tapes and gave them to someone else. Geoff Green didn't have them, so Keller's job is to make us tell him who has. He's already pumped us once."

"If you mean at the Hong Kong consulate," I said, "that didn't sound much like pumping."

"It did to me. I'm a very perceptive person—remember? He's asked me twice since then—when you haven't been around."

By urging Inada to phone Geoff from Hong Kong—by swearing we'd left tape recordings with Geoff in Duisburg—had I really signed his death warrant? Unless I could find a flaw in Candy's reasoning, maybe I was responsible for Geoff's death. I swore under my breath.

"Are you starting to believe I might be right?" she asked.

"I'm not sure. It's all guesses."

"That's why I couldn't put it into words before. It's easier now."

"Not for me it isn't."

"If I am right, there's not much left to find out," she said. "Not now we're sure the bomb was in the concrete plug. Don't you think it's funny Keller phoned to tell you?"

"Not if he wanted to reinforce his credibility. He'd have guessed Tegholm would let us know, otherwise he might have kept quiet about it." My words conveyed an unconscious acceptance of Candy's suspicions.

"He isn't risking much. You and Tegholm were in the cavern when it happened. You said you saw where the blast came from." She smiled. "You kept on saying it, all night long."

"I'll show you exactly where it was," I said. "Forget about

Keller for a moment. Apart from vapour vents and the manhole, there's only one other hole in the cavern. That's where the pipes go through the roof." I drew the three pipes on my picture.

"How big a hole?" Candy asked.

"No idea. Big enough to get the rubble out during the excavation. I couldn't see properly because it's been blocked up after the pipes were installed. It's just a bloody great plug of solid concrete."

"Not quite solid," Candy said. "CCC's explosives are buried inside it somewhere."

"Right. Just like they were in the foundation of the Rochling compound. Nice and simple, isn't it? Inada's never used any clever equipment—just a system for remote detonation and some explosives that won't deteriorate with age. Then he waits for wet concrete and a dark night."

"I wonder if my father knew," Candy said quietly.

"My guess is that he did. You said he went to lots of places where there'd been explosions and fires. He'd have noticed the craters were all in concrete. We've travelled halfway round the world to get an answer but the proof was right in front of us in Duisburg."

"Think of all the other bombs CCC haven't used yet," Candy said. "It's scary, isn't it?"

"It's more than that. Once you start thinking about it you can't stop. Inada's probably got explosives planted in structures all around the world. It's so damn simple. No matter how tight security is eventually going to be on a project, no one bothers until construction's got to a stage where there's something worth while looking after. Concrete foundations don't count. You can build a nuclear reactor, a hydro dam or a skyscraper with just about zero site security at the beginning of the project. All CCC has to do is choose the jobs that'll give them the biggest payoff and get in early."

"They have to wait a long time for customers, though," Candy remarked. "Years and years sometimes."

"It's called a long-term investment strategy," I said. "For all we know CCC's buried a couple of charges underneath the Sydney Opera House. I wonder who's going to pay to have that blown up?"

She frowned. "We still don't really understand how CCC makes the explosives happen, though. We're only guessing about that."

"It's got to be high-frequency radio pulses," I said. "All you need are receivers that'll reliably work after being buried for five or ten years in concrete."

"We should've figured the bomb was in the plug," Candy said. "Your mole couldn't have burrowed through solid rock, could it?"

I shook my head. "It'd be interesting to find out how long the charges have been there."

"I know when the Hjartholmen cavern was finished," Candy said. "Tegholm told me. It was 1977."

"So CCC were here in 1977. Right around the time the concrete was poured round the pipes."

Tegholm's construction records would tell us the exact day but the information was valueless. Records wouldn't tell us whether a second bomb was concealed somewhere in the plug. Even if the X-rays showed something—what then? Unless we could get at it to deactivate the fuse, CCC could fire the charge any time they liked. I remembered Inada saying CCC had two million dollars riding on the contract and he wasn't about to let that slip through his fingers.

"Okay," I said slowly. "I guess we can't take the chance on Keller. I'll have to speak to Tegholm and find out what he knows. If we don't do something, Keller could be helping CCC to blow Hjartholmen to pieces. There'll be the biggest oil fire in the whole bloody world."

"We're not telling anyone," Candy said stubbornly. "We

can't stop it from happening. Either the Swedish government agree to mine their uranium or they say good-bye to
the island. There isn't anything we can do. It doesn't matter
if Keller's double-crossed us or not. It doesn't even matter
whether you believe me."

I stared out of the window at the street below where the
citizens of Gothenburg were hurrying about their business
with their collars turned up against the cold. Somewhere
among them were two men who had come to this quiet
Scandinavian town on a mission of blackmail and destruction. Inada and Tadashi—men who, at the flick of a switch,
could not only create an explosion of truly unimaginable
proportions but men who could also destroy an entire island. And for what? The answer stuck in my throat. Geoff
was dead, Rochling was crippled and Keller might have
betrayed us. Only Candy was left.

I looked at her, wishing fervently it hadn't had to be like
this.

"It goes on, doesn't it?" she said gently.

"What does?"

"Everything, you and I, all this. We can't get away from
ourselves. It's a roller coaster we can't get off."

I continued staring out of the window.

"Why does Tegholm think there's another bomb?"
Candy asked.

I answered without turning round. "Everyone believes
yesterday was just a warning—a demonstration to twist the
government's arm."

"Why wasn't there a fire or a huge explosion?"

"Because there wasn't enough air in the cavern to mix
with the vapour coming off the oil. Tegholm only lowered
the level a few hours before we went in. CCC knew there
wouldn't be a bang. Perhaps Keller told them. He stayed by
himself in the pump house when we were in the cavern."

Candy came to stand beside me. "So if the government doesn't give in, they'll try again?"

I nodded. "And next time it'll be for real. The people out at the island won't be able to stop it. At some point the vapour-air mixture will become potentially explosive. According to you, Keller's out there right now doing his calculations."

She took my hand and held it tightly. "And it's no good pumping water in to fill up the store?"

"No. If the cavern's full, any sort of explosion will blow the roof right off it. There'll be an enormous avalanche of rock into the oil and plenty of oxygen. That's a recipe for a giant surface fire."

"So there really is nothing anyone can do?"

"No." I looked at her sideways. "Unless Tegholm can dig the bomb out of the concrete or unless someone finds Inada and Tadashi in time."

Candy was attempting to build an argument based on the fact that I was powerless to prevent the inevitable. Her logic was unassailable but both of us knew it didn't make any difference.

I interrupted before she could launch the punch line.

"The refinery people think Keller's out there helping them," I said. "We have to talk to Tegholm and find out whether he is or not."

She shook her head. "Even if you can make Tegholm understand, Keller's not going to stand around while you ask questions."

"I'm going to have a go, anyway. You know why."

"Yes." She sighed. "Oh, yes. I know why."

"There's Geoff Green," I said.

"To add to your list or have we got round to talking about good old-fashioned revenge now?"

I let go her hand and retreated from the window.

"Where are you going?"

"To get a drink." I opened the fridge and found a miniature bottle of scotch.

"It's nine o'clock in the morning."

"I know."

She came to stand in front of me. "Paul, don't."

I wanted to throw the bottle at something hard. I needed
to see the glass shatter and watch the liquid splatter out
over the wall. Instead I stretched out my arm and let the
bottle drop into the wastepaper basket. This time my fingers weren't trembling, they were shaking. Tegholm had
over a hundred men on the island—more by now. And if
and when it happened, every one of them would die.

"I'll make coffee," Candy said. "There's an electric kettle
in the cupboard. You go and get dressed."

When I was in the bedroom the phone rang again.

"Who is it?" I called out.

"The desk downstairs," Candy answered. "There's a
message from Tegholm."

"Get them to send it up."

She appeared in the doorway. Her face was pale.

"I've already asked them to."

"Okay."

We stared uneasily at each other.

"I'll go to Hjartholmen with you," she said.

I didn't say I wouldn't leave her here by herself and I
didn't say I was going to make her stay at Tegholm's main
office in Gothenburg.

There was a knock on the door.

I went to get Tegholm's note wondering why he hadn't
telephoned instead.

A second later I knew why.

There wasn't a note. And Keller wasn't out at the island.

He was here. So were Inada and Tadashi.

FOURTEEN

We were pushed downstairs at gunpoint. Three armed men to escort us from the hotel to wherever it was we were being taken.

No one in the lobby gave us a second glance, and although Inada's precautions to conceal his gun were rudimentary, the doorman even opened the door for him as we were led outside.

Insensitive to the cold and stunned by what had happened, I stood beside Candy while we waited for Tadashi to get the car. Candy had been right. From the very beginning Walter Keller had used me as a cover. The two weeks I'd spent at the Rochling depot, the night of the fire, his visit to my hotel the next morning and his sudden arrival at the Hong Kong consulate—elements of a plan to blame me for the Rochling fire and later to discover whether Candy and I had told anyone what we'd learned about CCC.

In Ireland I'd been betrayed by a man who for fourteen weeks had risked his life beside me and now another man I'd trusted had played me for a sucker. The bitterness was made worse by knowing it must have been Keller who'd murdered Geoff in Duisburg.

I was going to kill Keller. The resolution was intuitive and so intense that if Walter Keller could have looked inside my heart, he would have abandoned his mission and left Gothenburg on the next plane. Before he could destroy the caverns and destroy the island I was going to tear out his throat with my bare hands. The adrenaline was pumping and there was a dangerous singing in my ears.

A black Citroën pulled up at the kerb. Tadashi got out and came across to us. He left the engine running.

Inada said something to him briefly in Chinese, then turned to speak in English to Keller. "Are you confident you can handle this alone?"

Keller's face was drawn. "I was not aware of an alternative."

Inada ignored the remark. "You have brought the draeger equipment?"

"I have a gun, the radiotelephone and the draeger equipment," Keller answered curtly. "I shall make my first call in exactly sixty minutes." He inspected his watch. "At nine twenty-seven—although I doubt if it will be necessary for you to be ready for some hours yet."

"Harwood," Inada said. "On this occasion you will travel in the same car as the girl. You are to drive. Keller will accompany Miss Stafford in the back seat. The implications will be obvious to you."

I didn't answer him. Neither Candy or I had spoken since Inada had appeared at the door of our hotel room. The shock at seeing him again had proved curiously slight—either because of the sedatives I'd been given the night before or perhaps because somehow or other I'd always believed our paths would cross again. Candy had gone white but she too was visibly less frightened than she'd been in Germany or Hong Kong.

"Where are we going this time?" I asked.

"You know what a draeger tube is used for, Mr. Harwood," Keller answered. "I taught you to use one. You know very well where we are going."

"Good-bye, Harwood," Inada said. "And good-bye, Miss Stafford." He moved the gun in his pocket.

I shrugged, then went to the Citroën, climbed behind the

wheel and slammed the door. The fog from my brain had gone. Not since the fire in Duisburg had I been able to think with such remarkable clarity and not since I'd left Germany had I been so sure of what I was going to do.

When Keller and Candy were installed in the back seat I wound down the window.

"You're wrong," I said to Inada. "Right now you think you've won but you're wrong. You're finished, Inada. I'm going to see you burn in hell."

His face was expressionless when he answered. "Your words are more appropriate than you imagine, Mr. Harwood—regrettably they apply not to me but to you and Miss Stafford." He turned and walked away.

"Drive directly to the island," Keller instructed, "and drive with care. You may have guessed I have little to lose. If necessary, I shall kill Miss Stafford without compunction."

I neither understood nor cared how much he had to lose, but Keller knew and I knew I wouldn't take the chance on Candy.

"What about Geoff Green?" I said. "Was that without compunction or just for kicks?"

The Citroën was rolling now and I had Keller's face framed in the driving mirror. He'd started to answer me but changed his mind and clamped his mouth shut.

"Come on, Keller," I said. "This is the final run, isn't it? You can tell us. You're going to leave us in the cavern when Inada triggers his bomb, aren't you? Tell us about Geoff—you said it yourself—what do you have to lose?"

"You are an impatient young man, Mr. Harwood. I had nothing to do with your friend's death in Germany. Whatever else I may be, I am not a murderer."

"What about the poor sods who died in the fire at Rochling?" I said. "Who the hell do you think murdered them?"

Keller was displaying an uncharacteristic nervousness

and he hadn't told me to shut up. He almost seemed prepared to talk.

"It was the Baader-Meinhof who shot Green," he said. "The same terrorists who paid the China Construction Company to destroy my oil depot."

By referring to the Rochling depot as his, Keller didn't sound as though he was particularly pleased about it. And why would he bother to blame Geoff's murder on the Red Army? Had we somehow misinterpreted Keller's role?

Like me, Candy had sensed that Keller was uneasy.

"Are you a member of the Red Army or have you always worked for CCC?" she asked.

Keller lit a cigarette before he answered. "I have never been a member of the Red Army, Miss Stafford. For the moment let us say I have been acting on behalf of CCC."

"A sort of subcontract killer," I said. "Inada's paying him to help blow up the cavern and get rid of us." I swivelled round in the seat. "There are over a hundred men on the island, Keller. You're really doing it in style this time, aren't you?"

"Tegholm will be told to evacuate his men," Keller said.

"But no one's going to evacuate us," I replied. "We're accidentally left behind in the pump house—right?"

"Paul," Candy said suddenly. "He's going to make Tegholm think it was you and I who pushed the button. Don't you see. That's what they want everyone to believe."

"Is that it, Keller?" I asked. "Is that what it's all about?"

He didn't reply.

Stopping the Citroën at the intersection with the main road which led to the island, I thought over what Candy had just said. Had Keller always intended to set us up? Was that why we'd been brought to Sweden in the first place—to make it appear as though Candy and I were working for the consortium who was blackmailing the Swedish government?

"Drive on, Mr. Harwood," Keller said. "It is most important."

"Not to me and Candy it isn't," I said shortly.

"Things are not that simple," Keller replied. "You cannot save the island. There is much you do not understand."

"Keller," I said. "For Christ's sake. What exactly is it we don't understand?" I engaged gear and pushed the Citroën out into the traffic. During the two weeks I'd worked for Keller in Duisburg I'd got close enough to think I could read him fairly well. My judgment had been fatally wrong but I could swear that for some reason he was trying to tell us something.

"Miss Stafford is correct. Inada means you to take the blame for what will happen here today—just as you have already been blamed for the Rochling fire. Miss Stafford's father conveniently provided the first link with the fire in California. In Germany his daughter is being sought in connection with the Rochling fire—and now, under an assumed name, she is here in Gothenburg. You, Mr. Harwood, a recognised explosives expert, are known to have been paid by the Red Army for assisting them in Duisburg. Now you too are here in Gothenburg."

"Is that why you helped us get out of Hong Kong?" Candy asked. "Why you came to Sweden with us?" Her voice was unsteady.

In the mirror I saw Keller nod his head. "That is precisely what I suggested to CCC. When it was discovered you had not drowned in Hong Kong, someone had to silence you quickly. The concept of exploiting your connection with the Rochling fire was attractive to the Chinese."

"So the story about a freighter picking up our bodies in Hong Kong was all lies," I said. "The Hong Kong police don't think we're dead at all."

"Neither the German nor the Hong Kong authorities believe you are dead," Keller said. "They will, however, be surprised to learn of your subsequent reappearance in Sweden. I need not tell you how it will be confirmed. Three hotel rooms in three countries—all containing identifiable fingerprints."

I could see now why Keller had wanted us in Sweden. Our presence in Gothenburg was well established.

Plenty of people had seen us at Hjartholmen and dyed hair and fake names wouldn't fool Tegholm if, after the island had been blown out of existence by CCC's explosives, someone showed him photographs of two confirmed terrorists, Candy Stafford and Paul Harwood. Our own enthusiasm and Inada's clever manipulation of it had made us the perfect scapegoats for the destruction of the Hjartholmen cavern.

"There weren't any tapes," Candy said bitterly. "You had Geoff Green killed for nothing."

"It is done," Keller murmured. "And soon all this will be over, thank God."

We were approaching the first of the new roadblocks Tegholm had set up. Ahead of us, two cars and a truck were being turned back by a uniformed guard.

"Show your passes," Keller instructed. "But say nothing."

Although we were still over a mile from the island, this was an opportunity to make a break. I wrestled with the jumble of facts and half facts trying to decide what I should do. What did Keller mean when he said we didn't understand? Was the fuse already timed to detonate? If so, what was the radiotelephone for?

I slowed the Citroën and held up my pass to show the guard. He glanced through the window at Candy and Keller, then waved us through the barrier of oildrums.

According to the conversation outside the hotel, Keller was to make radio contact from the island at nine twenty-seven. Until then, I reasoned, it would be foolish to make any sort of move especially this far away from the complex where I could achieve nothing.

Without doubt Keller was nervous. He was chain-smoking and nearly everything he said was defensive or apologetic. I had to pry more information out of him—see if I could discover more about the part he was playing.

"You don't have to kill Candy," I said. "Let her out at the main gate onto the island. Inada and Tadashi won't ever know." I avoided looking at him in the mirror.

"I do not wish to kill anyone, Mr. Harwood."

"Then stop the bloody thing right now," I said angrily. "What the hell's the matter with you, Keller? If you can stop it—stop it now."

"You do not understand. It is not your fault—it is mine."

"Try me, Keller," I said. "Just try. Explain, man—for Christ's sake, explain." I looked at my watch. It said five to nine. "Shall I turn the car round and go back?"

"No." Keller's face was flushed. "No, we must proceed to the cavern immediately. It is the only way."

His nerve had gone. For reasons I didn't understand Keller was unravelling.

"What is it you're supposed to do?" I asked quietly. "Tell me."

"Measure the concentration of vapour and air. The draeger tubes will tell me whether the mixture is already potentially explosive or whether Inada will have to wait for more air to leak in through the vents."

"And if it is explosive?" I said.

"Then I am to confirm by means of the radiotelephone."

"Like you did yesterday," Candy said, "when you tried to kill Paul."

"No, Miss Stafford. Yesterday was a warning to the government. I had already determined the mixture was safe. Today is different. The Swedish government has been as stubborn as the government in my own country. Today,

Inada and Tadashi will create an oil fire a thousand times more terrible than the one you saw in Germany."

"Then lie about the mixture," I shouted. "You don't want this to happen, Keller. I know you don't. Give us time to do something."

"I intend to lie," Keller answered. "It is a decision I made some time ago. But Inada no longer trusts me. He will have made his own calculations—I fear he will trigger the fuse despite what I may say."

My confusion was complete. Had Keller really lost his nerve or was this another twist in the convoluted trail that Candy and I had been following since we'd left Germany?

"I shall explain while you continue driving, Mr. Harwood," Keller said. "There is little hope, yet perhaps together we may be able to think of a solution."

Ten minutes ago he'd been threatening to kill Candy—now he wanted us to join forces with him.

"Explain what?" I said helplessly. "You've lost me, Keller."

"The details are unimportant and there is little time. I shall tell you only that I was first approached by Inada sixteen years ago in Germany when I was site superintendent for the expansion of the Rochling refinery. In return for a large sum of money I was persuaded to let the contract for the foundations to a Hong Kong company called China Construction. The bribe I received allowed my wife and me to purchase our own home and lead a very comfortable life we could otherwise never have afforded in Germany in those days. Naturally, I was aware of the dangers to my career if the truth were ever to be become known, but over the years I managed to convince myself that my dishonesty had harmed no one." He paused. "I was, of course, quite wrong. Four weeks ago when Inada came to see me in Duisburg the extent of my foolishness was made very clear. You can guess the rest, I think."

"I suppose Inada had proof of the backhander he gave you," I said quietly.

"Indeed he did. Deposit slips for my bank account and a recording of an unfortunate conversation in my office. For sixteen years Inada had been waiting to remind me of an indiscretion I had nearly managed to forget." Keller's eyes met mine in the mirror. "Inada said he had come to collect interest on the money he had paid me."

"So you knew where the bomb was all the time?" I said. "You knew damn well it was buried somewhere in the concrete. You hired me and Geoff just to make it look good."

"Not an easy choice, Mr. Harwood. You see, I could either implicate myself with CCC and risk imprisonment and the ruin of a lifetime's work—or remain silent and witness the destruction of Compound Two. Perhaps if the matter had ended there I could have endured the guilt, but of course it did not end there. Miss Stafford arrived in Duisburg and circumstances took a very different turn—not just for me but for Inada too. Before I knew it, you had shot Pang's brother in Krefeld and you and Miss Stafford were on your way to Hong Kong. When you telephoned me from there I realised the terrible train of events I had set in motion." He stopped to light a cigarette from the butt of the one in his fingers. "I travelled to Hong Kong in an endeavour to persuade Inada, Tadashi and Pang to abandon further attempts to kill you. Do you understand now?"

"You mean you've been trying to protect us?" Candy said in disbelief. "You've pretended to be working for Inada so you could help us?"

"I have also been endeavouring to save the Hjartholmen oil store, Miss Stafford. The mistake I have made is in trying to protect myself at the same time. Until today I imagined I could achieve all these objectives without implicating myself. I now know that is impossible. I intend to tell Inada he must wait to detonate his bomb and hope we can either flood the cavern with nitrogen or deactivate the fuse in time. As a result of a recommendation I made last night, Tegholm's men are already pumping in nitrogen to replace the air."

"So what's the gun for, Keller?" I said. "Why force us to come with you at gunpoint?"

He smiled weakly. "To demonstrate my good intentions to Inada and to guarantee you would accompany me to the island. I think you would not have come otherwise."

Keller wound down the window and threw out the automatic. "It was not loaded," he said. "Now, Mr. Harwood, we have approximately twenty minutes. What ideas do you and Miss Stafford have to offer?"

FIFTEEN

Halfway down the causeway leading to the perimeter fence, the Citroën touched ninety miles an hour. On the wrong side of the road, hurtling past an unbroken convoy of trucks, I kept my foot down and prayed we wouldn't have trouble at the gate.

The trucks were hauling nitrogen. Trucks and tankers from all over Sweden carrying vital nitrogen to the island.

At two minutes to nine, still on the wrong side of the road, I brought the Citroën to a shuddering halt outside the gate.

One of the guards recognised us. He began to lift the barrier.

"Where's Tegholm?" Keller shouted to him. "It is very urgent."

The guard pointed to one end of the island where twenty or thirty bulldozers and scrapers were working in the centre of a huge cloud of dust.

"We can't drive over there," Candy said. "It's all rocks."

"Go directly to the pump house," Keller said. "I must take a reading. That will tell us how much time we have."

I rammed the Citroën into gear and took off through the barrier. If Keller had guessed correctly—if Inada was going to push the button anyway—we had less than half an hour.

Tegholm hadn't messed about. Yesterday, the surface of the island had been a desolate wasteland—today it was crawling with vehicles of all shapes and sizes.

Immediately over the plug, bulldozers had already exposed most of the concrete and through the dust I could see

X-ray trailers and the generators that were powering them. In the distance, a twenty-foot-high wall of rubble showed how much rock had been pushed clear of the plug and parked ready on the concrete were batteries of mobile air compressors, a thousand feet of high-pressure hose and more pneumatic drills than I'd ever seen in my life. Years ago this had been a huge construction site and now the roar of diesels and the fumes from their exhausts had returned to Hjartholmen.

But this time there was a difference—Tegholm hadn't just requisitioned every piece of earth-moving equipment he could find—the army was here too. As well as the hundreds of uniformed men patrolling the area, armoured cars, tanks and personnel carriers ringed the perimeter fence.

"My God," Keller said. "How are we going to get all these people to safety?"

"We might not have to," I said. "What does Inada use to trigger the charge?"

"Radio transmitter," he answered. "But I do not know the frequency."

I stopped the car outside the pump house and got out. Although it was still very cold, unlike yesterday the sky was cloudless and the wind had dropped. To herald the improvement in the weather, seagulls were wheeling high above the dust cloud rising from the plug.

Heaps of empty nitrogen cylinders littered the parking area around the building.

"The air smells of oil," Candy said. She hadn't been allowed to bring a coat and she was already shivering.

"The smell is a good sign," Keller said. "The nitrogen is forcing air and vapour out of the vents into the atmosphere." He took the draeger hand pump and tube from his pocket. "We will go to the changing room at once."

"We'll never make it without breathing gear," I said. "Not

while they're flushing out the vapour. We'll be gassed the minute we open the manhole."

"I shall go alone," Keller said.

"No you won't," I told him. "We won't bother with dry suits—just masks and air cylinders. I know where they are."

Candy came round from the other side of the car and stood in front of us. Her lips were so cold that she had difficulty in speaking. "It's past nine o'clock," she said. "There isn't any point in finding out how explosive the mixture is. If it is, there isn't time to save the island—not if Inada and Tadashi go ahead."

Keller stared at the rubber bellows and the glass tube in his hand.

"Everything's up to you, Mr. Keller," Candy said. "You've got to make Inada wait—convince him the mixture won't explode unless he waits a few more hours. Give the nitrogen time to get rid of the air."

"It might be safe already," I said.

"I do not think so," Keller said grimly. "And I do not believe Tegholm will find the charge in the plug. In places the concrete is five metres thick."

Four men emerged from the pump house. Two were carrying breathing equipment. I ran to meet them.

"Do you speak English?" I asked quickly.

One of them nodded.

"What's the vapour concentration?" I said.

He looked confused and said something in Swedish to one of the others.

"Keller," I yelled. "Quickly, bring the draeger over."

At the mention of the word "draeger" the Swede showed signs of understanding. I pretended to squeeze bellows and inspect the chemicals in the tube.

"Ah yes," he said, nodding. "The gas is still dangerous."

Keller arrived with his draeger.

"It's okay," I said. "I don't need it. I've already got the answer."

"A bad answer?" Keller asked. "You look worried, Mr. Harwood."

"The vapour mixture's still explosive," I said.

"How long before the nitrogen makes it safe?" Keller asked the man I'd spoken to.

He shrugged and pointed to the mounds of cylinders. "We have worked for seven hours with the nitrogen. There is not enough, I think."

Keller thanked him, then stood looking thoughtful.

Suddenly there was no need to hurry. The caverns were ready to blow. The fate of the island rested on the decision of a single man and we had only a slim chance of influencing that critical last decision. No one but Keller could save the caverns.

"What's the range of Inada's radio transmitter?" I asked.

"I do not know, Mr. Harwood. He has been careful not to tell me such things."

"What about yesterday? Where were Inada and Tadashi when they blew the first charge?"

Keller shook his head. "I do not know that either."

Candy drove the Citroën over to where we were standing and wound down the window. She'd been sitting in it to keep warm. "What about telling Tegholm to move his road-blocks further out?" she said. "If he's got enough men, he could stop anyone getting closer than two or three miles. There aren't all that many roads."

"Too much open country," I said. "Roadblocks won't stop Inada. He's too smart for that."

Keller dropped the draeger pump and ground the glass tube under his heel. He was trembling, either from the cold or because he knew what the three of us knew. Everything depended on the call he was about to make.

"What does your watch say, Mr. Harwood?" he asked.

"Nine-sixteen," I said.

"And yours, Miss Stafford?"

"Mine's back in the hotel," Candy answered. "What are you going to say to Inada?"

Keller climbed into the back seat of the car. "What can I say? Only that he must wait for two and a half hours—perhaps I could persuade him to accept three."

"What's the bloody difference?" I said. "We don't even know if he'll believe what you tell him. He might decide to go now—blow you up with it, Keller. Had you thought of that?"

Keller nodded. "By now I am supposed to have locked you in the pump house, but it would be convenient for Inada if I were to die with you. We must prepare for the worst, Mr. Harwood. We must instruct Tegholm to clear the island. It is possible Inada will detonate the fuse at his own discretion."

"We'll try in the car," I said. "To hell with the rocks."

Candy slipped across into the passenger seat and buckled her seat belt. She smiled at me as I got in.

The Citroën was willing, and if an armoured car that chased after us, hadn't cut us off we might have made it.

Tegholm came over to discover what all the commotion was about. He saw Candy in the front seat and spoke quickly into his radio to tell the armoured-car commander to point his machine gun somewhere else.

From the sound of the Citroën's engine, I'd torn the sump out. The inside of the car was filled with dust, smoke and the deafening noise from the bulldozers that were working over the plug a hundred yards away.

"Good morning," Tegholm shouted through the window. "You are lucky not to have been shot. What is the hurry?"

"Get your men off the island," Keller shouted back. "There is not time to explain." He glanced at his watch.

"Radio your instructions immediately. It is possible the cavern will explode in ten minutes."

Tegholm looked as though he was going to argue.

I threw open the car door and jumped out. "Do it," I yelled. "Do it."

He hesitated, then began speaking urgently into his transmitter. The effect was instantaneous.

As one by one the engines died an uncanny silence descended over the whole island. The hiss of compressed air from broken couplings and the creaking of hot metal were the only reminders of the hammering roar of a moment ago.

Needing no second warning, men were running away from the plug towards the main gate. More men sprinted from the pump house and groups of soldiers were falling back to the perimeter.

The driver of the armoured car restarted his engine.

"Tell him to wait," I said to Tegholm. "He can take us with him."

Tegholm nodded, speaking over his radio again while he held up the palm of his hand.

Inside the car Keller was hunched over the radiotelephone. It was twenty-eight minutes past nine.

"You will please tell me, Herr Studer," Tegholm said. "I must know what has happened."

I stood between him and the Citroën to block his view of Keller. This was no time to arouse Tegholm's suspicions.

"We're certain someone from here has been leaking information," I said. "Keller's scared the bomb'll be triggered early—before you've got enough nitrogen into the cavern."

"But why now?" Tegholm insisted. "You are not answering my question."

Keller finished his call to Inada and came to my rescue. He answered Tegholm for me.

"If I am wrong I shall explain later," he said quietly. "If I am correct, there will be no need for explanations. Meanwhile I suggest we too move away from here."

Tegholm was far from satisfied. He went to the armoured car and spoke to the commander.

"What did Inada say?" I asked Keller.

"He asked me how long it would take me to check my reading and report back." Keller gave a wan smile. "It is a trap. I told him twenty minutes. You may begin the countdown, I think, Mr. Harwood. Ten minutes from now Inada believes I will be busy in the pump house. We have until then to clear the island."

"Okay," I said. "Let's get the hell out of here."

I led Candy over to the armoured car. "She's half frozen," I said to Tegholm. "Is there room for her inside?"

The commander understood English. He jumped down from the turret and helped me lift Candy onto a tyre so she could climb in through the hatch.

"We'll ride on the outside with you," I said to Tegholm. "Tell the commander not to hang around. We're sitting right on top of the plug."

At first it was so cold it was difficult to make my hands grip the steel handles on the hull but once we were under way the strain of hanging on brought back some warmth to my body. We lurched and bounced over the rubble surrounding freshly exposed concrete, heading for the road that led from the pump house to the main gate.

Once we reached the road and the going was smoother, Keller leaned across towards me.

"All the personnel are clear," he yelled. "Soon we too will be safe." His face was blue with cold.

I glanced back to see how far we were from the plug. The armoured car was travelling faster now and at this speed we'd be at the gate in no time.

My confidence was short-lived. The vehicle slowed and stopped in the middle of the road.

Candy's head appeared from the hatch. She was pointing upwards.

Ahead of us to the west the sun was glinting on the fuselage of a light aircraft. It was flying at an altitude of about three thousand feet and heading directly towards the centre of the island.

"What do you think?" I asked Keller. "Sightseers or a way for Inada to beat the roadblocks?"

Keller couldn't take his eyes off the plane. Like Candy and me he was willing himself to imagine who was in the cockpit. Tadashi at the controls and, beside him with a radio transmitter on his lap, Inada? Or a foolhardy Swedish pilot, homing in to take a closer look at the dust cloud?

"Mr. Tegholm," Keller said. "Radio instructions at once. That plane must be shot down. I will take the responsibility."

This time Tegholm had sensed the urgency and no one had to yell at him. His instructions were terse and effective.

Outside the fence, uncertainly at first, machine guns began stammering, their muzzles spitting skyward at the tiny aircraft high above the island.

The response of the plane dispelled any doubts I'd had. Executing a series of evasive curves as he started his run in, the pilot opened his throttle and commenced his dive.

Inada wasn't going to turn back—either because he thought he could get away with it or because he knew that one way or another this was CCC's last job. More guns had joined the attack but still the plane came on.

The armoured-car driver realised the danger. We surged forwards racing for the gate. I hung on, not believing the plane could have ever got this far.

It was almost overhead, when the world exploded.

Fourteen million cubic feet of incandescent vapour burst open the roof of the caverns in a column of fire that shot a thousand feet above the island. And out of the flames came burning rocks. A hail of giant oil-drenched rocks that were on fire. Immense rocks the size of houses that had been blasted outwards from the shattered cavern roof.

The first shock wave squashed me against the hull of the armoured car as it tipped over. Another wave followed it—a terrible wave of heat, scorching and searing everything in its path. It licked over my face and hands, then suddenly I was on the ground with rocks crashing all around me.

The column of flame was being sucked back into what once had been Hjartholmen. I watched the sky turn black with smoke, watched a mountain of froth erupt from the ground and saw the surface fire begin.

There was a glimpse of a tiny, wingless aircraft spiralling into the inferno, then millions of gallons of oil that had been churned into an aerated foam ignited in a single flash of light. Soon the horizon was nothing but an advancing wall of flame.

Flooding into ruptured caverns, seawater was displacing the oil upwards. The fire was sucking oxygen to fuel itself and travelling at enormous speed, while a tidal wave of burning froth had already engulfed half the island. A fire-storm wind began swirling round the armoured car.

I dragged myself to my feet and went to inspect the turret. The hatch was smashed but Candy was alive. She was bleeding from a cut above her eye but she was alive. So were the commander and the driver. I pulled them out and then went to search for Tegholm and Keller.

Tegholm lay twenty feet away, his head severed from his body by a flying rock. Of Keller there was no sign.

The driver found him. He had died instantly, crushed between the turret and the surface of the road.

I could hear the roaring now. In a few minutes the wall of foam and the flames would be upon us.

We retreated, shielding our faces while we staggered and fought our way against the wind.

From the gate, two cars tore down the road towards us. With the flames no more than three hundred feet away, hands bundled us inside and we were carried off to safety.

The great caverns of Hjartholmen were gone. With them had gone a whole island, millions of gallons of oil, an aircraft and four men.

Shortly before we reached the fence I saw the bodies of Tegholm and Keller overtaken and consumed by fire. Like Candy's father and like Geoff Green, they had died unnecessarily, victims of CCC's last and fatal mission.

Later, when I looked back from the causeway where the cars stopped to let us out, the sky was dark and black smoke billowed from an enormous oil-filled crater where an island once had been.

What had happened here would never happen anywhere again. By destroying the island, Inada and Tadashi had destroyed themselves. By perishing in the monstrous fire that they themselves had lit, they had freed the world from the spectre of disaster in the future.

A mile away from flames still roaring upwards from the crater, I stood alone with Candy knowing that what we had begun in Germany had finally finished here today.

EPILOGUE

Sometimes, on a warm summer morning, Candy and I get up early to watch the sunrise over the forest. There's no special reason why we do this—it isn't a ritual and it isn't ever planned. One of us simply decides, pulls back the curtains and goes to start breakfast.

Today Candy decided, cups are rattling in the kitchen and I can already smell the coffee.

Lying half awake and half asleep, content with the knowledge that the sun is shining, I refuse to remember what day of the week it is.

The peace has been a long time coming. In the months following the fire I'd waited for it, expecting it partly because Candy had said it would come and partly because it was owing to me.

We found the cottage and moved here almost as soon as we'd returned to West Germany. Travelling from Sweden as Hans Studer and Ingrid Klemm on the passports Keller had given us in Hong Kong, West Germany was a logical place for us to head for and, although we hadn't planned on staying in Europe long, it's a couple of months since we've spoken of moving anywhere else.

Our cottage lies twenty kilometres east of Stuttgart on the edge of the forest, a tiny one-bedroom place that was once a hunting lodge. We settled into it as though we'd always lived here, and once Candy's German carried us through the first month, the people in the village accepted us quickly enough. I even have a job—unwanted but necessary in the circumstances. I got it accidentally by repairing a neighbour's shotgun in exchange for a leg of venison. Already my reputation as a gunsmith has spread as far as Weizham.

And so, while Candy and I have waited for the memories of the Hjartholmen fire to fade, the weeks and months have passed and winter has come and gone.

Making the adjustment hasn't been easy. Four months ago the papers carried a story about a terrorist threat to Hong Kong's water supply. Mines had been placed under the Lo Wu pipeline, the papers said. For a week we waited for the phone to ring or perhaps for a car to arrive at the cottage gate. It took us a month to discover Pang had been apprehended in Hong Kong on the same day he'd made demands for money and that he'd been killed trying to cross the Chinese border.

Then, too, although it was what we'd wanted, there'd been the strain of learning to live with each other. In the early days both of us had been on edge and my drinking problem temporarily resurfaced. But that's a while ago—before the peace and before we'd proved the dream would work. Much of the summer still remains, we shall spend autumn and winter here in the forest—then it will be spring again.

About the Author

Colin D. Peel lives on a hilltop near Auckland, New Zealand, with his wife, six dogs, eight goats, two horses, three cows, a cat, and numerous chickens. An Englishman by birth and an engineer by profession, he has previously lived and worked in Canada and the United States before settling in New Zealand. When he is not writing books, Mr. Peel runs a small herd of pedigree Angora goats, breeds show-quality whippets, and spends a good deal of time restoring and driving a 1910-vintage steam tractor engine. He is the author of ten previous books. FIRESTORM is his first novel for the Crime Club.